ROSALIE AMBROGIO

Port Adventure

Kidnapped on Stewart Island

First published by FH Publishing in 2018

First edition

ISBN: 978-0-473-45665-8

This book was professionally typeset on Reedsy.
Find out more at reedsy.com

1

The Woman in the Window

If I had gone to the police a little sooner, or if I had made myself known to Mrs Livingston before all the trouble started, things would have been very different.

I had passed Rata House every day for months. Several times a day if you included scurrying past about 7.30 in the morning on my way there and flashing by in the bus on the way back from work. It was only when out jogging each day early in the morning that I really had time to look at it. It was officially an Historic Place, built by an early settler in the days when people had large families and armies of servants to look after them.

Rata House was set side-on to the street, so that the hugely ornate wrought-iron gates opened onto a wide drive leading to massive doors only partially glimpsed from the street. It was located in the Scenic Drive so unpoetically named the Town Belt, a huge semi-circle of native bush which surrounded the top part of the city.

The house itself had its share of native trees besides tall hedges and rolling lawns, and well-tended flower-beds. Naturally, the tree most in evidence was the rata, and one could imagine some adventurous and slightly disgraced Englishman landing here a century and a half ago, hewing out a place for himself and sparing the beautiful rata trees. Then bringing his romantic bride to a wild and beautiful land.

I pictured them, sitting in the rose arbor, holding hands, possibly awaiting their first child, trying to decide what to call their new home, spending hours discussing suitable names, or whether to give it a Maori or a Pakeha name, then one of them exclaiming, "Let's call it Rata House!" and the other delightedly agreeing.

The whole ambience of the place could transport even the most procaic person back in time, full of romantic imaginings.

There were many large bedrooms on top, and above them the attics and gables. There must have been lots of other rooms, too, because I counted twenty chimney pots. The windows were those round-ended ones such as they have in churches, and a verandah ran around the front supported by slender cast-iron posts branching out into elaborate scrolls.

Even though it was so well cared for I had always assumed it was vacant, with the owners perpetually travelling around the world acquiring priceless treasures to add to its lustre, so I got a surprise one day to see an elderly lady at one of the top side windows. It was broad daylight, brilliantly sunny, too, otherwise I might have thought she was a ghost, especially as her face seemed to float at the window. Neither of us smiled. I was embarrassed, peering through the hedge like a potential burglar, and I hurried guiltily away.

The following day I was jogging past again. I had Frey, a medium-sized black-and-tan dog with me. She belongs to a neighbour and is one of the chief reasons why I have kept up my jogging instead of it being just another fad. Another reason is Charlie, a larger dog, a cross between a labrador and a bull-terrier. He belongs to a different and unknown neighbour, but he arrives on my doorstep with Frey every morning at 6.30 a.m.

Well, as I say, the three of us, Frey, Charlie and me were running past one day and we saw the old lady at the window again. This time she waved a blue-veined hand and said, "Hullo." I couldn't hear her, of course, but I saw her lips move.

I waved back vigorously and the dogs stopped for a moment. The old lady smiled a little, in a way that suggested she was sort of out of practice, like someone who has no-one to smile at.

Waving and smiling at the old lady got to be part of our routine. Now that I knew it was occupied I no longer gazed covetously at the house. A couple of times I thought of calling in to see her, taking some flowers or a few cream cakes. I kept thinking I'd call one Saturday or Sunday morning just for half-an-hour. I'd march up the enormous drive and I'd ring the bell (would it resound sepulchrally through that enormous house?) and I'd say, "Hi, I'm Giselle Dougal. I've called to have a chat." Or something like that. But I didn't.

I thought she might resent the implication that she was lonely, and how embarrassed I'd be if she didn't ask me in, and I had to turn away clutching a pathetic little brown bag full of soggy cream-cakes. After all, I thought, if she had wanted to know me better she would have come down to the marvellous, important-looking gates and said, "Why don't you come and have morning-tea with me on Saturday, dear." Or struck up an acquaintance by admiring the dogs as many people did.

But she didn't invite me in, and I didn't invite myself. Even now, I wonder if things would have turned out differently if one of us had overcome our reserve.

One morning a few weeks after I first saw her, as was now my custom, I looked up and waved. I saw her even more briefly than usual, because Charlie ran out on to the road and I had to haul him back onto the footpath. Even so, I noticed the old lady didn't wave, and that she didn't look at all well. Of course, she always looked delicate, dessicated even, all white hair, faded blue eyes and wrinkled cheeks. Still, I'd guessed from the start that she was about eighty years old. However, she did say "hullo."

By the time I looked up again the old lady had disappeared from the window.

It wasn't until lunch-time that I thought about it again. We were particularly busy at work that morning, arranging several bus tours in addition to our other work. I work at Bennet's Travel Agency in Princes Street. There are only six of us in the Dunedin branch, a receptionist, two shorthand-typists, another travel consultant, myself and Mr Bennet.

We are all, for one reason or another, mildly in love with Mr Bennet. Why the others love him I am not quite sure. He is about fifty, short, bespectacled, and happily married. The reason I am rather in love with him is because he chose me out of forty-six applicants and at the close of the interview when he told me the job was mine he actually said, quite seriously, "It'll be a great help to have someone smart and attractive out there to meet the public." It doesn't sound much, I know, but I have three highly critical brothers and two parents who have never got over their disappointment at my having red hair. So we all work like donkeys for Mr Bennet. On this particular day we got the bus-tours all organised without our usual turmoil and I set off to meet Errol for lunch.

Errol is the same age as me and is studying law at Otago

University. He is not exactly my boyfriend but he is the closest thing I have got to a boyfriend. We do not often have lunch out, about once a week. We go out together on most Sundays, usually to the Dunedin Botanic Garden or the Dunedin Public Art Gallery or somewhere else that either costs nothing or very little. Errol practically never has any money, and I am saving for a trip overseas. However, sometimes we meet for lunch when one or the other of us is feeling affluent.

On the day I am speaking of we went to the Hogshead, a sort of superior self-service restaurant. We had finished our meal and Errol was drinking his draught beer and I was drinking my small bottle of DB Export when he said, "I went to a party last night. I met a girl called Tandy Williams. She says she knows you."

Errol always talks like that — as though I am going to deny everything. It's because he's studying to be a lawyer. He fancies himself as a Prosecuting Counsel.

I was a little miffed that he had gone to a party without asking me to accompany him, but I made no biting comment. Nor did I enquire where the party was at or whether he had enjoyed it. Instead I said, "I haven't seen Tandy since I was at primary school. She used to be deaf as a post."

"She still is," Errol said. "But she lip-reads. I found her very interesting."

In Errolese this means that she listened with minimum interruptions to everything he had to say.

"I also thought she was very attractive," he added. This meant that he had more than two drinks. All girls are attractive to Errol after two drinks.

After a moment I said, "When I first became friends with her I used to talk very loudly, and very slowly, accentuating all the consonants — you know, 'What time is it?' and 'Isn't it chilly?'"

Errol laughed. "With deaf people you are supposed to talk naturally, and look at them as much as possible." Trust him to know that. Tandy Williams was probably the first deaf person he had ever met. But he would have read somewhere or heard somewhere the best way to talk to the deaf. He files every bit of information away.

I lifted my glass to take a sip and I suddenly realised what with speaking of Tandy Williams and lip-reading that the old lady had not said "hullo" that morning — she had said "help."

"Errol," I said, putting my glass down, "say 'hullo.'"

He stared at me. "I'll say goodbye in a minute."

"No, say it. Say 'hullo,' I want to watch your lips."

He got quite self-conscious then, looking all around to see that nobody was watching us before he obliged.

"Now say 'help.'"

"Help," he said, giving me another funny look. I told him then about the old lady.

"I'm sure now that she said 'help,' and not 'hullo.'" I finished.

"It sounds pretty unlikely to me," Errol said. "After all if she needed help she would just telephone someone, not hang around at the window waiting for you to go flitting past."

Errol is not a receptive person. Sometimes he is really dreary and unimaginative. I decided a long time ago that I will never be one of his clients. Of course, if I have ever got lots of money to invest, or want to buy my own home, I might go to him. But not for problems — not if I get married and then want a divorce, or want to adopt a child, or somebody poisons my cat or anything like that. Not, in other words, for anything that requires a bit of empathy. I will find a lawyer who is charming and understanding.

Putting these thoughts aside, I persisted, "But supposing she hasn't got a telephone?"

"Of course she'll have a telephone," he said scornfully.

"Well, supposing she couldn't get to it. Supposing she's broken a leg or something."

"If she's that old there will be a district nurse or a Meals on Wheels person calling in every day," Errol said. "You don't want to worry about it." What he meant was that *he* didn't want to worry about it. "You're looking good," he said, partly because he wanted to change the subject, and partly because I was wearing a new short-sleeved suit of lettuce green linen with a navy blue long-sleeved blouse under the jacket. I also was using my one and only Hermes hand-bag, flashing it about a great deal, taking my handkerchief out of it at intervals, and rummaging about unnecessarily while I did so.

Of course, it would have been too much to expect a more flowery compliment. All he ever says is "looking good," or the highest possible accolade "looking great" after lengthy appraisal, like a judge at the Miss New Zealand Contest. He walked back to my office with me, chatting about his holiday job.

There were no clients to be attended to, so everyone was talking about an item of news that Rona, our receptionist, had just heard on the radio. Rona is the least busy of all of us. She can see out to the street watching everything that goes on and listens to her transistor all day. All telephone calls are passed on to one or other of the rest of us, and all clients are smilingly but hastily shunted our way. She doesn't do any typing, not even envelopes, because Mr Bennet has this theory that we must take responsibility for every aspect of our bookings. So Rona is always first with the news. Apart from that, her conversation is mostly about her boyfriends. She thinks she is better looking than Bo Derek.

"There's been another bank robbery," she said. "They think it's the same people who robbed the bank at Wakari yesterday. They tied up the tellers and scooped all the money into a green suitcase." She turned the volume up on the radio and we all listened eagerly as they repeated the news. Three people had broken into the bank in the early hours of the morning. As the bank employees arrived for work they were confronted by a masked armed man and directed to a rear room where they were ordered to lie face down on the floor with their heads covered. After the robbery they were freed by the bank's first customer.

Discussion of the robbery naturally turned into a discussion of what each of us would do if we had a lot of money, a conversation continued in snatches between bouts of working.

Immediately following afternoon tea I decided to post some mail. It's something I enjoy doing, as I gaze in all the shop windows and do all kinds of little bits of private shopping on the way. However, I was still thinking of what I should do about the old lady. Having been brought up to be a good citizen and a good neighbour, I decided to go to the police. Fortunately the police station was quite handy so I wouldn't be gone from the office long enough to arouse comment.

When I got there I went to a desk resembling the counter of a draper's shop, behind which several policemen, some in uniform, others in plainclothes, were standing.

It's a funny thing, but when I got there, it suddenly didn't seem important enough to report. Sort of like the way a toothache goes away when you get to the dentists, or you suddenly feel very healthy when you're sitting in the doctor's waiting room with a cough because everyone else there is either seven months pregnant or has two broken legs. I suddenly lost confidence. What exactly had I to report? Was I really there to say that an old lady hadn't greeted me as usual that morning? There were several other civilians there who I was convinced had just been burgled or had found a stranger hanging by his neck in the toolshed.

As I stood there, more or less rooted to the spot, all my confidence draining out of me, a policeman said, "Can I help you, Miss?"

When you are feeling confused and inferior you don't take much of a shine to anyone, but I don't think I would have much liked this particular man under any circumstances. He was young but he had an old and cynical manner clearly designed to trivialise anything reported to him. His face was as round as a tennis ball and his hair was the colour of butter. His eyes were that clear and inscrutable blue that apparently they issue with the uniform.

"Well," I mumbled, "I pass a house every day and the old lady who lives there always says 'hullo' to me and this morning she didn't."

There were other policemen standing about, doing things like answering phones, operating machines, talking. Suddenly I felt several pairs of inscrutable blue eyes on me. Were they thinking that I was having them on, taking the mickey, pulling their legs?

"I think she said 'help,'" I said.

"You heard her crying out for help this morning and you come in now?" he looked at his wristwatch. (Several weeks ago there was a paragraph in the paper about how two policemen had rescued an elderly woman's cat that was being chased by a dog. Everyone went around all day saying how wonderful the police are, and weren't we lucky to have them. I felt utterly certain this constable I was now talking to was not one of the two who had rescued the old lady's cat.)

"Well," I said, "I didn't actually hear her. It's just, you know, afterwards when I thought about it I thought, well, she had said 'help' and not 'hullo.'"

"What's the old lady's name?" he asked me, after a long, bleak pause.

"I don't know her name. I don't actually know her." I said, trying not to shrink. He raised an eyebrow.

"You said you didn't actually hear her. If you didn't hear what she said then what makes you think she asked for help?"

"Well, I never really *have* heard her. She's always behind a closed window."

"You read lips, do you?" he asked, with wonderfully offensive mildness.

"Well, yes I do," I said. "Sort of. I used to be able to."

He placed a sheet of paper in front of him. I had the feeling that he would throw it in the waste-paper basket as soon as I left. He did not sigh aloud, but one could see that he was sighing inwardly.

"Where is this house?" he asked as though by humouring me he would get rid of me more quickly.

"It's in the Town Belt," I said. "It's called Rata House." He began, somewhat resignedly, to write this down. At that moment one of the men in plainclothes came over and stood beside Fat-Face.

"Look, Peter," he said. "I'll take care of this. I'm Senior Sergeant Zoltan Baker," he told me. "Let's go in here and you can tell me all about it."

We went into one of those small rooms where I suppose they interview all the murky characters who frequent police stations. We sat down on opposite sides of a small desk and he moved a stamp pad away from me saying, "We don't want you to get ink on your nice green suit."

Then he asked me my name and when I told him he said, "Giselle? What a pretty name."

When I gave him my address he said, so pleasantly, "Oh, yes, I know Huia Avenue."

He couldn't have smiled more winningly if I had said that I lived in Buckingham Palace. In a way, it seemed just a short time that I was there.

It was quite nice really, sitting there while he listened intently, asking what I suppose were astute policemanly questions, showing his white, perfect teeth in frequent quick smiles. His eyes were the regulation blue, but twinkly and sincere and deep and misty like californian lilac. When he looked down I noticed that he had thick curly brown eyelashes, dusted with gold at the ends. His hair was as thick, curly and as brown as those lashes and as soft looking as a small boy's. When he turned his head for a moment I noticed that even his ears were perfect. I felt that I was falling in love. If he had asked me at that moment to throw caution to the wind and live with him in a log cabin in Nebraska, I would have gone immediately.

"So you've never been in Rata House?" he asked.

"No, I wish I had. I'm very interested in historic places."

"Oh, so am I," he said enthusiastically, mesmerising me again with that fabulous smile. "As a matter of fact I think I'm right in saying that it's owned by a Mrs Livingston. I'll tell you what I'll do, I'm going off duty now so I'll take a run up there and see that she's all right. Will that put your mind at rest?"

I nodded and we left the station together, I giving Fat-Face a stare of triumph from the exit door. He stared laconically back.

As Senior Sergeant Baker took his car keys out, I said, greatly daring, "I suppose I couldn't come with you?"

His eyes slid sideways for a moment. Was it against police regulations to take someone with them when they were on official business? Probably.

"I mean I may never get another opportunity to see Rata House again," I pleaded. Or you, you beautiful, perfect, marvellous, charming human being.

"I was just going to suggest it myself," he said, opening the door for me. On the way driving up High Street I enquired about his first name and he informed me that his mother was Hungarian and his father a New Zealander.

We turned into the Town Belt and in a few moments stopped outside Rata House. The massive gates were unlocked, but stuck with disuse. Senior Sergeant Baker thrust his massive shoulder against the inside edge of the left side and swung it open. I was impressed. We walked up the wide carriageway together, finally passing under a rose-covered trellis, like two lovers, and arrived at the front door.

A ship's bell, a genuine one (there could be nothing imitation in that splendid edifice), was attached to the side of the door. It pealed loudly when Zoltan Baker rang it. We heard footsteps, young, firm footsteps and we knew it wouldn't be Mrs Livingston who opened the door.

A young blonde man stood somewhat truculently before us. It seemed to be my day for meeting handsome men. He was tall and pale, with sculptured lips and very bright light eyes. Just as he was he could have made a fortune in films playing a

Hitler Youth or a Nazi Pilot. His expression was just right for the part too, remote and humourless, until he saw Zoltan and his eyes widened.

Zoltan said, immediately, "I'm Senior Sergeant Baker. This young lady is worried about the elderly lady living in this house. Her name is Mrs Livingston, isn't it? She says she didn't look too well this morning."

The young man continued staring in a baffled way at Zoltan, like someone who didn't speak English.

"I'm her grandson, Patrick Livingston," he said eventually. "She's all right."

"You won't mind if we come in and make sure of that?"

I was surprised. Wasn't Zoltan exceeding his authority by asking to see the old lady after being assured by a relation that she was all right, and that she was not on her own?

"All right," said Patrick Livingston ungraciously, holding the door wider.

We stepped into a hall that had a sort of waiting area off to the side.

"You wait here," Zoltan said to me, smiling but firm. "Where is she?"

Patrick Livingston led Zoltan up a wide stairway paneled with kauri which even in the old days must have cost the earth. I was left sitting on a pew also made of kauri and upholstered in rose velvet and black leather. I longed to take a peek around the house. I sat for a few moments and then crept over to look in what I correctly assumed was the lounge — sorry, *drawing room.*

I opened the door very quietly, ready to hop back to the velvet pew before they returned. There were two people in the room — a man and a girl. The man was clad in dirty jeans and a check shirt, the girl in skin-tight jeans, a sun-top and high-heeled sandals. As my grandmother would say, she looked as common as muck.

"Who the hell are you?" The girl asked. They couldn't have looked more startled if I had been a werewolf.

"I'm a friend of Mrs Livingston's, sort of," I said, looking guilty and apologetic. A carton of beer and several empty bottles stood on the highly polished table. They were drinking out of crystal glasses.

"How did you get in? Isn't that door locked?" the man said, with a great deal more alarm than the situation called for, I thought. After all, I am a very inoffensive person. I was quite pleased that Zoltan and Patrick Livingston had now come down the stairs and were standing next to me in the doorway, where I was poised like a startled doe.

"It's all right. Don't worry. She was worried about Granny. She went to the police. This is Senior Sergeant Baker. He's just been up to see Granny."

The man and the girl looked at each other and back at us. They said nothing more. They looked as baffled as Patrick Livingston had done when we first arrived.

Patrick Livingston showed us to the door. When we were outside Zoltan turned back to him and said, "I'm glad your grandmother's all right. Make sure you take good care of her, won't you?"

Patrick Livingston nodded bad-temperedly. Zoltan and I walked down the path.

"I didn't like *him* much," I said.

"Oh, why?" Zoltan asked.

"Oh, I don't know. I kept wondering where he was when Hitler needed him."

He laughed. "Can I give you a lift back to work?"

"Yes, please," I said. "I'm at Bennet's Travel Agency."

When we got back to town he asked, "Would you like to have a cup of coffee with me?"

"Oh, I'd love to," I said enthusiastically. Even though I never drink coffee, I would have drunk hemlock if it meant I could be with him a little longer.

We went to a coffee bar with largely glass frontages. It was uncomfortably near my office, in view of Mr Bennet's habit of rushing out of the office to do shopping in response to imperious telephone calls from his wife. Still, I *had* thrown caution to the winds.

He asked me lots of questions, about where our farm was and my flatmates, and what my hobbies were. It was the most wonderful ten minutes of my life, sitting there with the most handsome man in the world displaying all this keen interest, while I tried not to screw up my face as I sipped the unwanted coffee. I wished everyone I knew in the whole world would pass by and look in and see us together and be suitably impressed.

As it happened, the only person I knew in the whole world who did see us was Mr Bennet. He stared in at us in a significant way as he went by with his arms full of groceries. It was the stare of a man who was paying me to make money courteously helping people plan holidays, not to sit around chatting up men in coffee bars.

Zoltan Baker interpreted the look. "Your boss?"

"Yes, he's very nice, but he likes us to keep our noses to the grindstone."

"Well, I'd better let you go," he said, half-rising.

Never let me go. "Oh, it doesn't really matter. This *is* my coffee-break, anyway."

"Oh, that's all right then. I just meant I wouldn't want you to lose your job."

"They couldn't manage without me." I said.

"That's the spirit. How's your coffee?"

"Delicious." I lied. Zoltan paused for a moment.

"You have such beautiful hair," he said. "It's a lovely colour." And then, as though he had not said anything at all, he went on, "Do you miss the country?"

"I'm never homesick or anything, but I do miss my parents and my brothers," I answered quickly, ignoring the flush of heat in my cheeks.

"What are they like? Your family."

I strove to think of something interesting to say about my family. I couldn't think of a thing.

"Well, you know what Tolstoy said about all happy families being happy in the same way and all unhappy families being unhappy in a different way? I come from a happy family. It is not an aid to conversation. None of my brothers is a drug addict, my father doesn't beat my mother, my mother doesn't have boyfriends."

"Kind of boring for you," he said, with mock sarcasm.

"No, but kind of boring for other people. I mean, Rona, my friend from work, has terrible rows with her mother every morning. Mostly about where she's been the previous evening. Then Rona gives us a blow-by-blow account every day at work. And, my flatmate Christine hates her father so much she only goes home to see her mother when he's out. What's your family like?"

"The same as yours," he said, adding, "Would you like a cake or anything? I'm sorry I didn't ask you before."

We both peered into the little glass compartments on the

counter. The only things left were those grotty little cakes that always get left till last because nobody likes them and everyone wonders why anyone bothers to make them.

"I'd love one of those," I said.

He paid for it and brought it over to me. I ate it very slowly because it tasted as awful as it looked, and also to stretch out this wonderful encounter.

Zoltan Baker left me just before we got to my office. He didn't enquire as to whether he could see me again, but he knew where I worked and he knew where I lived, so I wasn't too dismayed when all he said was, "Well, goodbye, nice meeting you." I began immediately to wonder whether he was married.

Dunedin is a small enough city to find out about anyone if you really want to. Rona would surely be able to find out for me through her network of friends. If not, I could hang around the police station in a discreet sort of way.

After all, if his shift finished at 3 p.m. I could be sauntering past at the appropriate time, going his way on the same side of the street so that he would be obliged to offer me a lift. What could be more natural? I'm not really a man-chaser, but I thought he was the handsomest, most charming person I had ever met. I was also convinced he was one of the policemen who had rescued that poor cat from the dog. He just had to be.

When I got back to work Mr Bennet called me into his office and said: "I'd like you to go to Stewart Island tomorrow. I want you to stay at the new hotel complex."

I was shattered. Normally I look forward to trips away to report on new hotels and motels, or even on older ones that we have just contracted to send clients to. Mr Bennet likes to be able to say in hearty tones that "Our Miss Dougal was there recently and thoroughly recommends it." Unfortunately he didn't seem to feel this way about new accommodation in Hong Kong, England or America.

"You do want to go, don't you?" he asked, looking puzzled.

"Oh, yes," I said.

"Good. You can fly down and come back by sea and road, or vice versa."

"A good idea. Thank you, Mr Bennet," I said effusively. No good jeopardising any future trips to Singapore, Rarotonga, Budapest…

As I went out the door he said, "I didn't think you liked coffee, Giselle."

"I don't, Mr Bennet. It's the company I enjoy." I replied. I was busy getting my work up to date before five o'clock, so I had no time to nurture my disappointment at having to defer for a few days my plans to ensnare Zoltan Baker.

2

The Usual Suspects

As soon as I got home I rang the Pet Meals on Wheels and asked them to come and feed the cat for the next few days. The Cat sort of went with the house. He was sitting there when we first moved in and at first we thought he belonged to a neighbour. Despite our ceaseless overtures he was not a friendly animal. We tried to give him various names but as he ignored them all we ended up simply referring to him as The Cat. Although we fed him on good steak and gave him the top milk from the bottle he did not succumb to our overtures and showed a stoic indifference to our comings and goings. Christine installed a cat-door which we knew The Cat used in our absence, but if one of us was about he miaowed bossily so that one of us had to get up and open the real door to let him in and out.

When I say "home" I mean where I live in Dunedin. I share an old bungalow with three friends, Christine Peters, Tim Sutton and David Tallintyre.

Christine is vaguely related to me. A cousin of a second cousin. When we were children my mother sent her parcels of clothes I had finished with. I don't know if she was grateful at the time but she resents it now judging by her frequent barbed references to my being a rich sheep farmer's daughter. I easily counter this by remarking on how strange it is that bossy people always become nurses or teachers.

It was my mother's idea that she should be one of my flatmates, "You ought to have someone you know with you," she had said emphatically.

My only recollection of Christine from childhood was a very faint one of when we were both about seven and she had come to one of my birthday parties. She had been a fat, plain child who had snivelled all the time because I got all the presents, and then she had been sick all over the carpet.

When I first came to Dunedin we had arranged to meet, or rather our respective mother's had arranged for us to meet, at the City Hotel for lunch. I had got there first and was hanging about wondering if I would know her again after all these years, when I saw her approaching, fat, plain, and, something told me, ready to snivel at a moment's notice.

As soon as she saw me, she said, "I recognised you at once — you're still as skinny as ever."

I said, "Fat people always call slim people skinny. Now that we've got that out of the way let's go and eat."

Tim Sutton is an Australian whom Christine offered a lift as he was hitch-hiking around New Zealand. As far as I could gather she had picked him up in a little tearoom she always stopped at just out of Dunedin. She arrived home with him one evening a couple of weeks after she and I had moved in.

A rucksack and a sleeping bag were his only luggage. The way his thigh and calf muscles bulged beneath his brief shorts suggested he did more hiking than hitching. He was so casual and friendly that I liked him immediately. His wardrobe consisted more or less of what he stood up in, but he filled his room with expensive stereo equipment which he played with fearful loudness and never let any of us touch.

David Tallintyre was our third flatmate. Tim and our landlord met him in a pub a couple of nights after Tim himself had moved in, and told him we needed a fourth person to help with the rent. They brought him along to be inspected. I remember when I first met him how he looked very pale and slight standing next to Tim who was tall and tanned. David smiled all the time as he talked. I had never actually known anyone who could do this before except for television announcers, and I always thought they must have learnt how to do it at a special school. It was all the more noticeable in David as he seemed to have twice as many teeth as anyone else.

His accent was English so I asked him what he was doing out here, making conversation while Tim and Christine were in the kitchen making supper.

"Well, I've got a yacht so I've taken a year off work, and I want to spend some time sailing around your beautiful coast."

He made it sound as though I owned the entire country, coast and all. I couldn't resist saying: "You're pretty lucky to own a yacht and to be able to afford a year off work at your age."

David said, "Well, I've saved up for a few years to take the year off. As for the yacht, I was born out of wedlock and my natural father, who I never met, left me the yacht when he died. A fit of conscience, I suppose."

The old-fashioned phrase, 'born out of wedlock,' and his slight, appealing, diffidence made me decide he would be suitable, and he moved in that evening.

I had assumed that his remarks about being illegitimate were made in confidence, so I was surprised later to find that he had also told Christine and Tim. Not that it mattered. It just seemed like the kind of thing one might keep to oneself, for a while at least.

There had been trouble, of course, when my father found out I was mixed flatting. Not trouble exactly, but a few days after we had moved in my parents arrived with some trumped-up tale about having some business to attend to.

It wasn't that they didn't trust me, it was the unknown men they didn't trust. As my father was paying my share of the rent I couldn't object, although I had no real gripe. If my parents didn't care about me, who else should.

They had found us all in bed when they arrived unexpectedly one Saturday morning a few days after we had moved in — our respective beds, of course. We had been to see a play at the Fortune Theatre the previous evening and then we had sat up late talking, eating take-away chicken and drinking beer which David had bought on the way back. Tim drank his straight from the bottle, as he always did, which provided him with a logical excuse not to help with washing the glasses. With his beard and untidy hair, and the way he clutched his beer bottle with both hands he looked exactly like one of the brothers Karamazov.

My parents were genuinely embarrassed that they had arrived when we were not up. They explained that they had called early in case we were going out and hadn't wanted to miss us.

Apart from being a bit bleary-eyed to begin with, the day went off very well. We all received them in our dressing-gowns, with the exception of Tim who didn't own one. I don't think he owned any pyjamas, either, as I never saw any on the line when he did his washing. He put on his shorts and a khaki jersey.

My mother was greatly impressed by David's silk paisley dressing-gown and cravat. Everything about him was impeccable, his clothes, his diction, his manner. I'm sure my mother decided he would be too gentlemanly to take advantage of us poor girls.

As for Tim, he was more like a bad actor playing an Australian than a real Australian. He always called everyone "mate" (except my mother whom he addressed as "ma'am", which made her feel so like royalty that she took quite a shine to him, too.) Apart from that, he had such a nonchalant attitude, such an air of lazy harmlessness that nobody could imagine him making the effort to get a girl into bed with him.

We all drove down to Port Chalmers where David's yacht, *Neptune's Daughter,* was moored. We spent the day sailing.

My mother behaved ever afterwards as though she had been on a two week cruise on the Loveboat. Knowing her, it was obvious she would spend the next few weeks trying to persuade my father to get rid of our jet boat in favour of a yacht.

They went back to the farm after my father had taken us all to dinner at the Lucerna.

As they left my mother said to the two men, "It's so nice that Giselle's got such fine young men to look after her."

David replied, "It's nice for us to have Giselle and Christine to look after us, too."

My father liked Tim, and David too. Having spent the day observing us all bickering and laughing together any fears he had must have been allayed.

Viewed from the street the house is exactly like a child's drawing. It is painted white with a green roof and just in front of the matching gables, two exactly similar cypress trees rise with precision out of the cropped lawn.

It is owned by Mr Leo Thompson, a short, heavily built man of about forty-five. He has a square face which ought to give him the appearance of openness and honesty, but a lipless avaricious mouth and very low brows over small pebble-coloured eyes make his general appearance that of a fairly good-looking orangutan. He speaks in a soft posh voice and has a smooth manner.

Instead of allowing us to post the rent he insists on calling for it each fortnight "to see if anything needs doing," as he puts it. We have always been amused by this remark because when the washing machine broke down, and another time when the fridge began defrosting when it wasn't asked to, he took weeks to fix them.

I have this belief, which Errol tells me is quite irrational, that people who don't like animals can't be trusted.

Mr Thompson doesn't like The Cat. The first time he saw it he asked, "Is that your cat?"

"We don't know whose cat it is," I replied. "We don't even know it's name."

"I don't allow any pets on my properties," he said, pursing his lips till his mouth disappeared completely.

When he had gone, Christine, who had not spoken up at all, said, "You are a liar, Giselle."

"I am not a liar. I may sometimes be a bit devious when necessary. Anyway I don't think people should be able to rent out properties and then tell other people how to live. We're only his tenants. He hasn't adopted us."

"Oh, he's quite a nice chap," Tim had said. "What have you got against him?"

The boys liked Mr Thompson, largely because he sometimes invited one or both of them out for a drink. Christine liked him, too, simply because he was a man.

Oddly enough, he had never noticed the cat-door, or if he had he hadn't mentioned it. Perhaps he thought if he acknowledged it he would have to remove it and in spite of his frequent visits he wasn't looking for work.

It wasn't often that we were all at the house together. Christine's job as a public health nurse for outlying areas took her away for days at a time. Tim used the house as a base in between setting out for sight-seeing trips to various parts of the country, and David, of course, was away on his yacht a great deal.

David was my favourite flatmate. He was more like a polite guest than one of us. When Tim took us on an outing, as soon as we got home he divided the cost between the four of us to the last cent, and we all had to cough up our share, but David always waved away any contributions from Christine and me. Also he was less apt to try to get out of doing the dishes than Tim, and he took us sailing in his yacht frequently, sometimes just for the day, more often for entire weekends.

The yacht, an ocean-going keeler, was pretty impressive; all chrome, polished wood and cerise sails. It transpired that Tim and Christine had been boaties all their lives, but I hated the sea. I went with them on their trips partly because they were fun to be with and partly because it impressed my other friends.

David became a different person on the yacht. From the moment he put on that peaked cap and pea jacket he behaved like Captain Bligh, bellowing orders and generally treating us like lower-deck scum. He had the best sleeping accommodation and the rest of us dossed down where we could, after much argument.

I spent the early part of that evening watching television

with a tray on my knee with The Cat for my only company. My thoughts were mostly of Zoltan Baker. The projected trip to Stewart Island now seemed like a blessing in disguise. I reasoned that if Zoltan Baker wanted to see me, either for personal or police reasons, and I was not to be found, surely his interest would be piqued.

I decided I would take my own car in the morning instead of going by bus or rail. It is a Fiat Bambina which my grandparents gave me for my eighteenth birthday in the hope, not yet realised, that I would visit them often. This meant that I could wear my new jeans and a shirt and change into something else later in the day, as I had decided I would call in and see my parents on the way down to Bluff seeing as their farm is on the way.

About nine o'clock, just as I was reflecting about them all, I heard a key turn in the lock, and recognised David's footsteps.

"Hullo, all on your own?" he said by way of greeting.

"I'm glad you're back. I'm off on a trip in the morning. Just for a few days. I have to report on a new hotel."

"A nice perk for you," he said, looking pleased and impressed.

"If you're going to be here you can feed The Cat. I'll cancel the Pet Meals on Wheels."

"I'm not certain of my plans. You'd better just leave your arrangements as they are."

"Oh, all right. It doesn't matter. It's just that while I'm on Stewart Island…"

"Stewart Island!"

"Yes, why?"

"Nothing, really. I didn't know they had a new hotel there."

"Yes, and a very posh one."

He poured himself a whiskey from our drinks cabinet, and stood studying me.

"David," I said, after a moment. "I've thought of a wonderful idea. Tim and Christine will probably be back by Friday. Why don't you bring them down for the weekend and meet me there?"

The idea did not appeal to him, quite obviously.

"I was thinking of going to Oamaru," he said.

"The fishing's great at Stewart Island," I coaxed, "and the scenery's terrific."

He hummed and hawed, but finally he said he might come, and he might bring Christine and Tim. Just then, the door opened and Christine herself came in, with a handkerchief clutched in her hand.

"I didn't expect you back until Friday," I said.

"I've got a dose of the flu," she said. "I might take a couple of days off."

Being exposed constantly to all those germs certainly hadn't built up any immunity to them. She succumbed to every virus she met.

Her current boyfriend, Gary Sinclair, was an intern at the Dunedin Public Hospital. He was thin and exhausted looking and looked as though he suffered from a lack of every known vitamin. Neither of them was much of an advertisement for their professions. They did not discuss their patient's ailments, they discussed their own.

"If you are feeling better by the weekend, Christine, perhaps you could come down to Stewart Island. I'm trying to persuade David to come down there."

"Why?" she asked, sitting down, one hand to her forehead, trying to look as wan as possible.

"I'm going down to look at the new hotel," I said. "I might get bored not knowing anyone."

"I can't think why you don't get a more useful job," she said.

"Tourism is our fastest-growing industry," I replied importantly.

"Can you make me something to eat?" she asked.

"I will if you persuade David to come down to Stewart Island and you come too, if you don't die in the meantime."

"Oh, could we, David?" she asked him.

"We'll see. We'll see," he said, smiling and seeming preoccupied.

When I lay down that night, I fully expected that I would dream of Zoltan, but it was Mrs Livingston I dreamed of, and she was still calling for help.

In the morning I took the dogs over to the park on the upper side of the Town Belt. People tell me that I am very sentimental about animals and that this is very rare in someone who comes from a long line of farmers. All I know is I felt quite sad that I would not see the dogs for a few days and I thought lugubriously of how they would wait in vain for me for several mornings running.

There are bellbirds in the park and there is one of whom I am particularly fond. It whistles so cheerily, its voice chiming in the air. Months ago I got into the habit of stopping not far from the tree it favoured and whistling back at it, not very melodically, I'm afraid. Still, the bellbird seemed to enjoy it, for it waited there, it's glossy purple neck swelling with song at our approach. It had a sense of humour too. Bellbirds are great mimics. Sometimes it would whistle in exactly the same way that I whistled to the dogs to get them to stop or come back to me. The dogs got quite confused sometimes and the bellbird hopped about a little on its high branch, greatly amused. On this day the bellbird whistled alarmingly and when I looked up I saw a furtive figure crossing the park just past the skate-board dip. I am woefully short-sighted. It took me some time to figure out who it was walking towards me, his air of sly menace souring the brilliantly sunny morning. It was the man who had been in the lounge at Rata House with the blonde girl.

Of course I gathered the dogs quietly to heel and fled into the thick forest at the edge of the park even before I knew who it was. Nobody knows the park and its environs as I now do, after months of playing hide and seek with the dogs and retrieving countless sticks and balls.

I hid behind a pohutukawa tree that was dropping its red blossoms on the grass. I watched the man hesitate, peering in various directions, looking for me. Obviously his eyesight was not a great deal better than mine. Then he hurried off confidently in the wrong direction disappearing behind a clump of huge lime trees.

The dogs thought it was a new game. They didn't make a sound.

After a cautious wait we went home, with much backward glancing, and I deposited Frey at her house and Charlie headed off around the corner.

The others were out already, Tim and David probably on the way to *Neptune's Daughter* and Christine to her mother's or to work. The sooner I could get away the better I would be pleased and I prepared a thermos and some sandwiches, flung them into the car, got in myself and drove off.

3

Beware Blue Eyes

The journey to Mataura was soothing as I took the peaceful coast road. It wasn't long before I was able to convince myself, not that I hadn't seen the sneaky little man in the park, but at least that he hadn't been as menacing as I had imagined. You know how it is when you want to minimise a feeling of danger and do not wish to appear hysterical. You play everything down, rearrange the sequence a little, rationalise. After all, I asked myself, why shouldn't that man have been in the park? Didn't he have as much right to be there as I had? Just because I didn't like the look of him didn't mean he should be prohibited from using it. It is a *public* park. He was staying for the moment in a house not far away. Surely it was perfectly natural for him to be walking there?

After stopping at the side of the road on the way through the rainforest to eat a belated morning tea, I sped on to my parents farm.

Experience has taught me not to send prior notice of a trip home. My mother worries that I will have an accident and my father hangs about waiting for me at the top of our road, pretending to be mending a fence, a job he never does himself anyway.

When I arrived we had a good lunch and all my father's employees came over to see me briefly. They all think my job is a bit of a joke anyway, but when they heard I was being paid to spend a few days on Stewart Island they could scarcely believe it. The idea of somebody paying for my opinion of a new hotel caused a great deal of unrestrained merriment.

My brother Alistair was down on holiday from the University of Manawatu where he is taking a degree in Farm Management. When I arrived he had gone into Mataura but he came back while we were all sitting on the lawn. He leapt out of the car and rushed over to kiss me. My brothers have become very affectionate since we all left home.

"I had to back up when I turned into our road," he told my father. "Two people in a car said they were lost."

"Where did they think they were going?"

"Well, they said they were going to Invercargill."

"How could anyone make a mistake like that?" my father asked.

"What kind of a car was it?" my mother asked.

"A Falcon, red," Alistair said.

"I wonder who they were?" my mother said.

I lay back on the grass and closed my eyes against the sun. It was like old times hearing them. In the country any unusual event, however trivial, is the subject of much discussion and speculation. I listened with amused tolerance. I was a townie now.

Alistair had persuaded my father to buy a helicopter.

Ours isn't the kind of farm where a helicopter is at all necessary, but although we have in certain respects been strictly brought up, our parents have tended to indulge us in many ways. It wasn't until I left home that I had realised this.

Alistair took me flying in the helicopter for a few hours, letting me take the controls and teaching me, more to show off than to please me.

Afterwards, he and I took some .22 rifles from the house and did some target practice. Years ago my father had painted a large boulder as a target for us. Of course, my father and brothers shoot rabbits, but my mother and I never do. Even if I had never read *Watership Down* I still wouldn't have shot them.

My father was always explaining to me the harm rabbits did. Once I informed him, very grandly, that "I may have been brought up a Christian, but by temperament I'm a Buddhist." But he was not prepared for a philosophic discussion, and his only reply was, "You talk like a damn fool sometimes, Giselle. Go and help your mother to get dinner ready."

Later, when I went to my bedroom, my mother followed me in for "a talk." We always had "a talk" when I went back to the farm. The thing is, my mother married at eighteen and she thinks of me as a twenty-three-year-old spinster. She is torn between the desire to have me safe at home and the equally strong desire for me to be out in the world looking for the "right man." We have seriously conflicting ideas about who the "right man" will be. If, for instance, I had told her in advance of this present visit, she would have rounded up every available land-owning bachelor of Protestant beliefs in the South Island. I don't know how she finds them. It amazes me that someone who gets around as little as she does can know of everyone's movements for hundreds of miles around.

I began to comb my hair. My mother stood behind me, smiling confidingly into the mirror. She put a hand on my shoulder and asked, "Have you met any interesting people lately?"

For "people," read "men." I was longing to talk about Zoltan.

"Yes, as a matter of fact I met a very interesting man just yesterday."

A gleam, excited and predatory, came into her eye immediately.

"What's his name?"

"Zoltan," I said. "Isn't it nice?"

"Where on earth does he come from?" She cried. "What kind of a name is that?"

"It's a Hungarian name!" I told her.

"Hungarian!" she said, abruptly sitting down on the bed. She has the most transparent face. Obviously she had some pretty wild ideas about Hungarians. I could see that in her mind's eye a picture of a lecherous folk-dancing peasant was vying with that of a sinister communist spy.

"Oh, Mum." I said, going over to her. "He is from here — his father is a New Zealander. And besides I've only met him once, for about three-quarters of an hour."

"Where did you meet him?" she enquired, sure that I had been frequenting sordid Bohemian dens.

"At the police station!"

She had been about to rise from the bed. Now she sank back on it.

I said quickly, "Look, I went down to report something, and that's how I met him."

I told her then about Mrs Livingston. Ordinarily she would have been very interested in this episode, instructing me to keep an eye on Mrs Livingston in future and reproaching me for not having done so sooner. My mother does not comprehend the difference between country ways and town ways. But for the moment her attention was fixated on Zoltan.

"So he's a policeman then?"

"More like a detective," I said. "He wears plainclothes."

I could tell that she was trying to figure out how much he was likely to earn and what his prospects were.

"Mum," I said, very, very firmly. "Remember I only met him yesterday — for *less than an hour.*"

"But he asked you to have coffee with him," she declared.

"That is hardly a declaration of love," I pointed out.

"Well, dear, all romances start out like that, with small things."

"Yes, I suppose that's true," I said, turning to the mirror. "You know Mum, he admired my hair. He thinks it's beautiful."

This was the wrong thing to say. When my mother was young, girls were supposed to be five feet two, have eyes of blue, and be either very blonde or very brunette. I have grey eyes and am five feet seven. My mother considers she has borne a giantess.

She looked at me sideways again. "He doesn't mind your being so tall?" she asked.

"Mother," I said. "I am only average height. It is a very fashionable height. I do wish you wouldn't keep trying to undermine my confidence."

She sprang up, hurt. "You know how much we all love you," she said, "I am not trying to undermine you. Goodness me, everyone knows that a girl doesn't have to be pretty now."

What kind of a remark is that to make?

She went to the door, turning back with a conspiratorial wink and a smile. "We won't tell your father and the boys about Zoltan just yet."

I sat down, closed my eyes and sighed with exasperation.

We had crayfish and vinegar sauce for dinner, in my honour.

We all went to a tin-canning in a neighbour's barn in the evening. We drove fifty miles to it and everyone I'd known since childhood was there. The young couple who had just got married were both friends of mine. There was heaps to eat and drink and the dancing ranged right through from ballroom to punk rock and square-dancing.

Unfortunately we had to leave early because my father was going to drive me to Bluff the next morning to catch the *Wairua,* the ship that would take me to Stewart Island, at 8.10 a.m..

I hate getting up in the middle of the night. We breakfasted, very early. My mother was quite happy she would see me in a few days time as I was going to call in at the farm for my own car on the way back to Dunedin.

We made good time, and I slept part of the way. Then we stood watching the vehicles loading on. The passengers waited on the wharf. I had taken a motion-sickness tablet. My father had the goodness not to notice. There was something unmentionable about a travel consultant getting travel-sick.

Foveaux Strait, known for being rough and unpredictable, stretched in front of us. I had made that crossing before. It lasts 2 and a half hours but it seems like a lifetime to those who have no Viking ancestors.

As always there were masses of people on the *Wairua.* Stewart Island is the most southerly of the three main islands of New Zealand, and is a great deal smaller than the North Island and the South Island. It has an irregular coastline indented with many bays and inlets, and several natural harbours.

The chief commercial industry is fishing, and there is a thriving tourist trade. The coastal forest scenery is magnificent, and the bird life — some of it unique of its kind even in New Zealand — is famous for its friendliness. Tourists stay at hotels, motels and camping grounds in their thousands in the season. They walk, boat, swim, fish and birdwatch during the day and in the evening attend lectures arranged by the Forest Service or relax in the hotel bars or on the beaches in the last rays of the sun.

Just before it was time to embark my father said, "There's a red Falcon. I wonder if it's the same one Alistair saw yesterday."

"Could be. They may have just stayed in Invercargill overnight," I said, although I thought it unlikely that it was the same car. Red Falcons are pretty common.

I kissed my father goodbye and boarded. I waved as we pulled out to sea. I had a cabin number. Most people don't use their cabins on such a short crossing but I went down to mine thinking I would feel better down there. While lying on my bunk wishing the ship would sink I noticed the door handle turn. I had locked the door but I realised three other passengers would have right of access to my cabin as there were three other bunks. I lurched off the bunk and opened the door. There was no-one there. Still feeling sick I decided to go up on deck. Perhaps the wind on my face would make me feel better I told myself, knowing it wouldn't.

I stood by the edge of the deck. I noticed blearily that one of the rope links was not fastened as it should have been. There were dozens of people milling about on that part of the deck. Below me was the deep grey tumultuous sea. I felt a sharp nudge in my back. I grabbed the side reflexively but would have gone straight over the edge if not for a powerful middle-aged seaman who grabbed me by the arm and pulled me, squawking horribly, back over the side. He had seen that the rope link was undone and was just heading over to see to it as I went over the side. People gasped. Some women screamed. They took me down to give me a cup of tea. Even the Captain came to see me. I assured him I was perfectly all right, although my arm felt as though it had been wrenched out of its socket. He said he would buy me a drink when we got ashore.

At last, at last we arrived at Stewart Island. The Captain enquired where I was staying and I told him.

"The Rakiura, oh, I believe it's pretty posh up there. If you wait until we are unloaded I'll give you a lift."

We all stood about while they got the suitcases off. They came ashore in crates and then everybody dived to retrieve them.

The Captain came over to me. "Which is yours?"

"That blue coloured one," I said, pointing.

"Very nice," he said. So it was, too.

"It's what all the best travel consultants are using this year," I said.

When he came back with my case he said, "So, you are a travel consultant? Who are you with?"

"Yes, I'm with Bennet's."

"Go on," he said, nodding his head slowly to indicate he was impressed, although Bennet's is small and fairly new, and he had probably never heard of us.

We got into his car and we were at the new hotel in ten minutes. He was a nice man. Not very old, but his manner to me was fatherly. He was probably thinking I could have drowned falling off of his ship. He told me the job as captain of the *Wairua* was only temporary as the usual captain was on holiday.

The hotel was, as he said, "pretty posh." The architects had made a great job of ensuring it suited the landscape. It was long but not high. Only three storeys. The windows were floor to ceiling, and the drapes were of some stylized Maori design. Downstairs were the kitchens, the dining rooms, the dance-floor, various bars and of course the offices and reception area. The two upper storeys were accommodation.

"Let's hope you've got a room overlooking the sea," the captain said, as he parked his car.

"I've got a suite," I said, mock-snobbish.

"Well, let's hope you've got a *suite* overlooking the sea."

"I hate the sea," I told him. "I get awfully sea-sick."

"Doesn't that rather spoil the image of a globe-trotting young travel consultant?" he asked.

"It would if it were generally known," I said, giving him a sideways look. "It's a well-kept secret. I suppose that's how I nearly fell off your ship — I felt so dreadful. I must have nearly fainted."

The Captain parked his car and we went into the hotel. He stayed in a small bar, sipping a whiskey while I went upstairs to change.

My suite was beautiful. The furniture was of colonial design and made from rimu. The ashtrays were paua shells set into heavy black bases. Not heavy enough to stop them being pinched, I thought. There was a fireplace of Oamaru stone and a mantle-piece on which there were two more or less matching lumps of red volcanic glass. A large carved panel depicting a Maori god clutching a mere, or club, glared down at me with its paua shell eyes. The ceilings were glazed in a dimple finish and there were so many mirrors and so much glass that everything shimmered madly. You could go back saying you had enjoyed yourself even if you didn't step outside.

I went into the bedroom, unpacked quickly, showered and dressed. I had brought a pale pink sleeveless dress, bloused at the waist, with me. It was casual but expensive. Pink is my lucky colour.

I went downstairs to join the Captain. He stood up as I approached the table and asked me what I was having. There were no waiters in this small bar.

I'll have a vodka and lemonade with ice, please," I said.

It amused me to watch him go to the bar and back with his rolling sailor's gait.

I said to him, "Do you ever get sea-sick?"

"I have done," he said. "But I have found a cure for it."

"Really? What is it? Stay on dry land, I suppose."

"No. Just drink a glass of sea-water."

I was screwing up my nose at the very idea of this when a man walked through the door and up to the bar. With his drink in his hand he turned nonchalantly around and then, as they say, our eyes met. It was Zoltan Baker.

In that first second when I saw him come in it actually seemed too wonderful to be true. My heart gave a great lurch at the sight of him. For a moment I thought the combination of the travel sickness tablet and the vodka was making me hallucinate.

I gave Zoltan such a delighted smile that the captain, who had his back to him, turned his head. He must have been as surprised as I was when Zoltan put his glass down, glanced furiously at me and immediately left the bar.

"A friend of yours?" The Captain asked.

"Certainly not," I replied.

"He didn't look too pleased to see you," The Captain persisted, enjoying himself.

"You noticed that too, did you?" I said, getting quite ratty.

He laughed heartily, thinking Zoltan was a boyfriend with whom I had had a tiff.

"Well, you'll soon make it up. He's hardly likely to be jealous of me."

"And why not?" I said, with spirit. "I don't see anything remarkable about him."

The Captain continued to be amused about the incident until he left quarter of an hour later.

"If there's anything I can do for you while you're here, just let me know," he said, giving me his phone number.

I stood at the door and watched him go, and then I walked dispiritedly back to my suite.

A bellbird, alighting on one of the trees in the grounds stared cheekily in the window, reminding me of my bellbird in the park. Had he missed me that morning? Or was he like Zoltan Baker, moody, unpredictable and insincere. I did not know whether that bellbird was male or female. I had never seen it up close enough to decide. In spite of their beautiful songs they appear quite drab in their olive green plumage. The males have a slightly brighter colour and more of that glossy purple round their necks. The females have a white streak curving down from the base of the bill to below the eye.

I had often thought of taking my binoculars to the park one day and establishing the sex of the bird, but had resisted the idea of adding any impedimenta to my morning run. However, I reflected bitterly, if the bird behaved in a huffy, bad-tempered, ill-bred way for no reason at all when I next saw it, I would know it was a male.

I went down for the second sitting for lunch, having resisted the temptation to skulk in my bedroom.

Fortunately, two very friendly Canadian girls were seated at my table. They were quite excited because they were going to see a Maori lady who was renowned as a psychic, to have their fortunes told.

"Why don't you come, too," one of them, whose name was Sally Vercoe, said. The other one, a pretty blonde, was called Marilyn Taylor.

"I've only been to one fortune-teller," I said, "and everything I was told was either trivial or ambiguous or both. You know — I was getting a letter, going on a journey, meeting a dark man."

"Oh, do come. It's such fun," Marilyn said. "It's such a lovely walk too. We went up last night to make the appointment."

One thing I didn't want was to be seen mooching around on my own by Senior Sergeant Baker, as I now haughtily thought of him, so I agreed to go with my new Canadian friends.

Mrs Rahine, the psychic, lived at Ringaringa, so it didn't take us long to get there, just past Lonnekor's Bay and over the hill. The abundant native ferns and brush were alive with birds, and fat wood-pigeons, always in pairs, stared down at us. The male birds, much bigger than the females, were touching in the way they frequently turned to gaze fondly at their mates.

I was able to identify some of the trees, rimu, rata, manuka and inaha. Sally and Marilyn were quite delighted to find Canadian maples and Australian blue gums.

Certainly the walk was beautiful. We had all changed into shorts and blouses so that we could get our legs browner.

Mrs Rahine lived in a small cottage on a very large section. The section was very overgrown in spite of the heroic attempts of a horse and fat lamb grazing on it. She came to the door and instead of inviting us in she suggested that we might prefer to sit out on the lawn in the sun. We did just that. Mrs Rahine parked her ample bottom on a large tree stump and we sat on the quite long grass in front of her like three disciples before a guru. Her voice was a hoarse croak, and she waved her pudgy hands a lot while she talked. I was disappointed that she was merely going to read our cups as any European psychic might have done. Somehow I had expected her to use some peculiarly Maori way of divining our futures, like rattling some moa bones, or selecting pieces of flax in a Maori version of the I Ching.

We drank our tea out of enamel mugs and handed over five dollars each. Just briefly I wondered whether Mr Bennet would consider this a legitimate business expense.

Mrs Rahine read Marilyn's cup first, then Sally's. They seemed to be very impressed, hanging on her every word — obviously she was telling them what they wanted to know.

Then it was my turn. Mrs Rahine peered at the tea-leaves, then she looked at me with her liquid but piercing eyes.

"There is a man with blue eyes — don't trust him."

I nodded in spite of myself, thinking it was a pity someone hadn't told me that a couple of days ago.

"You are in very great danger," she said.

The Canadian girls looked at me with new interest.

Mrs Rahine continued, "This man with the blue eyes, he pretends to be what he is not."

How true! How true!

"Always remember that the sea is your friend," she said, rather mysteriously, and apropos of nothing at all.

I did not trouble to point out to her that up to now the sea and I had not been on very good terms.

Mrs Rahine plied us with home-made biscuits while we listened to her. If her psychic abilities were half as good as her cooking then we all had happy futures, apart from the present danger she had indicated to me. She had a habit of saying each word separately in a staccato bark so that with her hoarse voice it was like talking to an angry walrus.

All three of us had been told that we would be happily married within the year. As Marilyn was sporting a small but twinkling engagement ring and Sally, besides being very attractive had a look of eager availability about her which some lonely bachelor was bound to notice soon, I didn't think she had to be very clever to say this.

We said goodbye to Mrs Rahine and began our walk back to the hotel.

"Wasn't she marvellous?" Sally exclaimed.

"I don't wish to appear cynical," I said, "But what did she really tell us? She told us we were all going on a journey across the sea. Well, she probably knows everybody who lives on the island. We have to cross the water even to get back to the South Island. And you two have very pronounced Canadian accents, don't forget."

"But she told us we would all be married within the year," Sally said.

"True, but she would have noticed Marilyn's ring, and in any case we are all at the age where it's obvious we will probably get married soon."

"Oh, you are a wet blanket," Marilyn said, "What about your being in danger. What was that about?"

"Don't ask me," I said, "I'm in no danger."

The girls were not staying at the hotel. They were camping and had merely gone to the hotel for lunch as a special occasion as they were leaving Stewart Island the next day. They had already been here a week and it was time for them to be moving on.

Out of gratitude to them for befriending me I invited them to be my guests at dinner. They were quite thrilled.

"We might even meet our future husbands," Sally said, giving me a waggish jolt on the arm.

I took them to my suite to get tidied up for dinner. Because they were casually dressed I told them they could borrow some of my clothes to wear to dinner, as we were all roughly the same build. Everyone was expected to tart themselves up for dinner, although you could go into breakfast and lunch dressed any old way.

Marilyn chose a blue-bloused sheath with spaghetti straps. Sally wore my lettuce green linen suit without the navy blue blouse, and I wore a white dress of lace cotton that I considered made my hair look more auburn.

We all traipsed down to the dining room. The crowd was very cosmopolitan, if not very young. I doubted if anyone under 30 could have afforded to stay in this hotel. There were many Japanese, including a camera team who were making a publicity film for their tourist industry, and some unusually unassuming Americans, botanists, who were studying the unique flora of Stewart Island. We got all this information from our chatty waiter. There were Germans and Italians and, of course, a few Englishmen who I had seen earlier in the day looking very self-conscious in their shorts.

It was obvious from the menu that the hotel was going to specialise in New Zealand foods, and wines. There was toheroa and oyster soup, whitebait, lamb done in a variety of ways, wild duck, venison, mutton bird, kiwi fruit sitting on large slices of pavlova, and so on.

It was all very good so we tucked in. My broken heart was not affecting my appetite. After dinner we went into the lounge for coffee and liqueurs. It was absolutely full to capacity.

"It looks as though *all* the guests have taken pity on waifs and strays," I joked.

"Don't look now, but the most gorgeous-looking man is coming our way," Sally said.

I was determined not to look. The men in the dining room may have been rich, and intelligent, but none of them was gorgeous-looking, so I wasn't surprised to see Senior Sergeant Baker standing at our table.

"Good evening," he said, looking directly at me.

I went quite pink, to my fury, but I managed to say in a coldly puzzled voice, "Good evening."

He raised one eyebrow at me, then he turned his charming smile on the girls.

"Would you ladies mind if I joined you?" he asked.

Of course they both fell over themselves to make room for him. I could have kicked them.

He sat down, saying, "Aren't you going to introduce me to your friends?"

"I'm awfully sorry," I said, very politely, "but I'm afraid I can't remember your name."

"I'm Zoltan Baker," he said in his engaging way to Marilyn and Sally. His smile was like an Eveready battery — it never failed. They eagerly introduced themselves as I had known they would.

The three of them sat chatting about the hotel, how good the weather was, how wonderful the scenery, how terrific the food. I noticed him stealing anxious looks at me, so I affected to be stifling little yawns.

"Tired?" he asked.

"No, just bored," I replied.

"That's a very nice suit you're wearing," he said to Sally, giving me a quick roguish smile which I ignored.

"Thank you," she said, simpering like a fool.

"There's dancing in the next room," he said. "Would you girls like to go in?"

The others jumped up eagerly, clapping their hands girlishly, and tossing their long hair about a great deal.

"I'm not coming," I said flatly.

"Oh, do come," they all said, making me sound like the local spoilsport.

"Oh, all right," I said, scraping back my chair crossly.

Zoltan found us a table and brought us all a drink. "A DB Export for you?" he asked after Marilyn and Sally asked for whiskey sours.

I refused to be flattered. After all it was his job to remember things.

After we had all sipped our drinks for a few minutes, he asked me to dance with him. For a brief moment I thought of refusing which would have meant sitting there watching him gliding past with Marilyn or Sally, drooling up at him. I preceded him with dignity to the edge of the dance floor. The band was playing a waltz, in deference to the elderly or the romantic among the dancers, I suppose.

He took me in his arms, holding me against his massive chest. His shoulders were so broad I couldn't see a thing if I looked straight ahead. When I looked up I could see his poreless Hungarian skin, the pink flush of health under the golden tan of his cheeks. He danced well, as in my dreams I had known he would.

"You dance well," he said.

"So I am always being told."

"That must be very gratifying."

"Not really. I never confuse compliments with praise." I said.

"What a very wise girl you are," he said.

I gave him an oblique look, which was all I could manage without cricking my neck, intended to convey contempt. He looked down at me with his Californian lilac eyes. I was deeply aware of the warmth of his body, his hand in the small of my back, and the light grip of his other hand on mine as he guided me around the floor. He was so fit, so strong, so tall, so well-scrubbed and clean-cut that any woman dancing with him would have been conscious of his magnetism.

I found myself wishing that the dance would never end.

When it did, all the other couples began milling their way back to their tables.

"Let's have the next dance," he said.

We stayed on the floor holding hands until the band started playing again. It was a foxtrot. Much as I enjoyed rocking and bopping, this was much more romantic.

I think he gave me a small kiss on my temple. We seemed to be dancing a lot closer this time.

"Tell me something," I said. "Are you going to ignore me the next time we meet?"

"Oh, you mean this morning. I've been meaning to speak to you about that," he said. "I apologise, I had a lot on my mind and it was a surprise seeing you down here."

Anxious as I was to forgive him this sounded a bit feeble.

"It was a surprise for me to see you, too, but I still managed to say 'hullo.' It was rather humiliating, your not even speaking."

"Look, I really am sorry," he said earnestly. Then he said, "Who was that guy you were in the bar with?"

Did I detect a note of jealousy? The Captain would have been flattered.

"He's the temporary captain of the *Wairua*."

"How do you know him?" he asked.

I was not about to admit to Zoltan (he was Zoltan again now) that I had been so sea-sick that I had nearly fallen off the *Wairua*.

"I know lots of people," I said. "As a matter of fact I met him this morning on the *Wairua*."

"I was on the *Wairua* this morning," he said, looking puzzled. "I didn't see you."

Naturally I did not admit that I had spent most of the journey sprawled on my bunk.

It was time to go back to our table. The band was now playing disco music, strobe lights flashing. Just before we sat down with Sally and Marilyn, Zoltan said to me, "There's just one thing I'd like to know."

"Yes?"

"Who owns the green suit?"

"I do," I said, laughing.

Both the girls were pleased to see us getting on so well together. Like the Captain they seemed to think that we had a big thing going before we re-met on the island.

After Zoltan had danced with each of them he suggested that we all go down to watch the mutton-bird coming in.

"What is a mutton-bird?" asked Sally.

I am not a paid-up member of the Forest and Bird Society for nothing. "It's a type of petrel, also known as a sooty shearwater. They lay their eggs on that group of small islands in Halfmoon Bay and some others." I pointed in the general direction of the Muttonbird Islands. "They spend all day at sea fishing and then return to their burrows when they have eggs or young chicks there, as they now have. They come in at dusk in a great cloud, hundreds and thousands of them."

We all set off towards the entrance to Paterson's Inlet. Hundreds of other people were walking the various tracks to different vantage points. The friendly American botanists were proudly escorted by about twenty people from the hotel.

After we had stood about for a while we saw the vast dark cloud of mutton-birds approaching. Even in such great numbers there is nothing frightening about them, not to my way of thinking, anyway. Individually they are shy-looking and very homely. Their colour is dark grey and they have an inoffensive cast of countenance. To many people the taste of their salty flesh is a great delicacy. The Maori, or part-Maori, are the only people allowed to hunt them in the hunting season which is in April/May, and some years a quarter of a million mutton-birds are killed and sold.

Nobody was killing them now, fortunately, and we all stood to watch them approach. Finally they plopped down in a most ungainly fashion and disappeared into their burrows.

As we were walking back to Halfmoon Bay, Zoltan said, "Let's all have coffee or something stronger in my suite."

Marilyn and Sally were very pleased and agreed at once.

I was surprised that he had taken a suite. Most single men would have simply taken a room, especially at such an expensive hotel. My mother would be relieved to know that he could afford the best. It was different for me. Bennet's Travel was footing the bill.

"You must be very rich," Sally said, rolling her eyes and smiling flirtatiously at him.

"No," I answered for him, smiling back. "Just a poor hard-working policeman."

He looked momentarily annoyed, I thought, because I had told them what his job was.

It was decided in the end that we would have the drinks in my suite as the girls had to give me my clothes back, and put on their own casual gear.

When we were sitting sipping coffee and eating brownie biscuits, Sally said, "How long are you staying here, Zoltan?"

"Oh, five or six days, perhaps more."

"Are you on holiday or working, or what?"

His eyes slid sideways for a moment. "I've got a few days off work, but of course if there was any trouble down here with the holiday crowds or anything I would be expected to turn to it."

"You mean with drunks and so on?"

"Yes, anything like that."

"I wish we were staying longer," Sally said. "But we are leaving in the morning."

"What a shame," Zoltan said, as though he really thought so. Did he have to be that charming, to everyone, all the time?

"Still, Giselle will be here," Marilyn pointed out.

"Yes, how long are you staying?" he turned to me.

Mr Bennet had given me to understand that he expected me back in a few days. However I had no intention of leaving before Zoltan did if I could possibly help it.

"Well, I'm supposed to look at all the things tourists do on the island. That should take a week at least," I said, trying to look very conscientious.

"Perhaps we could go somewhere tomorrow for the day?" Zoltan asked.

"I'd like that, thank you," I said.

Zoltan and I walked the girls back to the camping ground.

I had told them to visit my parents and given instructions on how to find the farm. While they changed back into their shorts in the bedroom I had asked them to tell my mother I would probably see her in a week's time, and not in a few days as I had originally told her.

When we got back to the hotel, holding hands and talking, it was fairly late. He left me at my door and went to his own suite further along the corridor. I had half expected him to kiss me goodnight, but he hadn't. I put this down to maturity on his part.

4

A Knock at the Door

As soon as I woke up in the morning I telephoned Rona at her home. It seemed wiser to let her inform Mr Bennet when she got to work that I might not be back for a week as I thought he might hum and haw or even worse, order me to get back sooner than I now intended.

"Hullo, Rona, it's Giselle," I said when she came to the phone. "Will you tell Mr Bennet not to expect me back for about a week, please."

"I bet you've met a man down there," she said instantly.

"Don't be so silly," I said stoutly. "I've decided to stay longer because there are so many things to do on the island. A few days is not nearly long enough."

"But you've been there before," she point out. "Anyway, it's only the new hotel you are supposed to be checking out."

"Rubbish," I said. "It's much better if we can tell the people in detail all the things they can do here."

"Why don't you ring Mr Bennet and tell him yourself?" Rona said.

"He won't eat you. Anyway, I am going on a launch trip and

it leaves before the office opens." I said.

"We're very busy just now," she said.

"Well, in that case you can pitch in and do some real work for a change," I said, as I quickly hung up.

Zoltan knocked on my door about a quarter of an hour later and we had breakfast together. We were among the first in the dining room and although there were two more chairs at our table nobody else sat with us. It was a good breakfast of porridge and cream and enormous quantities of blue cod and toast and jam and marmalade. When he was ordering he asked, "Coffee for you?"

"No, tea, thanks. I loathe coffee," I replied emphatically, immediately blushing. After a moment's puzzlement, he laughed.

"I've booked us on a launch trip to Ulva Island," he said, pleased with himself.

My heart sank. Despite what I'd told Rona, I was hoping to avoid going on boats for the time being. Still, I did have my motion sickness tablets. He correctly interpreted my glance out at the waves of the bay, which today were blue and placid.

"You do want to go, don't you?" he enquired considerately. "You don't get sea-sick or anything, do you?"

"That'll be the day," I said scornfully, adding quickly, "Mind you, I feel very sorry for people who do."

The hotel provided us with a packed lunch and we went down to the jetty, I having quickly swallowed a tablet.

From the moment we stepped on the launch I felt sick. The smell of the boat, the saltiness of the air, the lapping of the waves is anathema to me. Many people have told me that motion sickness is all in the mind, that I should think of something else, breathe deeply, chew barley sugar, and so on and so on.

Curiously enough it is always people who have never been sea-sick who have great faith in all these cures.

Everyone on the launch was very friendly in the way people on holiday in a confined space are. Zoltan did all the talking for both of us. I watched the shags, the gulls and the penguins glumly. Even the mollymawks, the poor members of the albatross family, did not interest me greatly at that moment, although when I was a child we had nursed one with a broken wing back to health, and I had taken a proprietorial interest in them ever since.

The other passengers were enjoying themselves, pointing at this, exclaiming over that. The owner of the launch cut the engines before we got to the Sailor's Rest, a pretty little cove, and we all hopped off. Thermos flasks were produced and everyone began to drink tea or coffee and eat their sandwiches and scones. The owner of the launch pushed his way towards me with a steaming cup in his hand.

"Have some beef tea," he said, "settle your stomach."

"Thank you," I said humbly. It was real beef tea, not just a melted cube and water, and it tasted beautiful.

Zoltan, who was deep in conversation with a middle-aged American lady whose teeth I noticed were as white and perfect as his own, pretended not to notice.

We wandered around Ulva for a while. The launch owner gave a short talk about the flora and fauna and then people wandered away briefly in twos or threes. The American lady, apparently travelling on her own, came with us, Zoltan taking my arm very solicitously.

On the journey back I watched the shore of Stewart Island and counted the seconds. I was violently sick over the side about half-way. It was a very calm crossing. Nobody else was sick.

When we got ashore and the first flood of relief at having reached dry land had subsided, I felt rather humiliated and certain Zoltan would not want to take me anywhere again.

However, he put his arm around me saying, "I can see why you have such sympathy for those poor people who get sea-sick, even though you don't."

"I suppose I looked dreadful,"

"Don't you know that Samuel Butler said people look very holy when they are sea-sick?"

"Isn't it awful? You know I actually fell off the *Wairua* yesterday. Or very nearly. One of the crew grabbed me as I was going over the side."

He stopped, I had not expected him to be so concerned.

"How could you possibly have fallen off?" he demanded. "How did it happen?"

"Oh, I don't really know. I was feeling sick and I was standing near the gangway and that bit of rope, you know that they use as a gate, was undone and someone in the crowd on deck just accidentally jostled me. I went right over but a great big seaman grabbed my aim and hauled me back."

He was frowning. "You could have been killed."

"Oh, I don't think so. I am a far better swimmer than I am a sailor."

Dinner was still a long way off. In spite of the fact that I wouldn't have minded a rest in my room I agreed to go for a walk to the lighthouse with him. It wasn't as warm as it had been so I changed into jeans and an intricately-patterned pink angora sweater. When I opened the door to the corridor he was waiting for me, so eager, friendly and alert that he reminded me of Charlie waiting on the doorstep every morning.

"What a pretty sweater," he said immediately. "Did you knit it yourself?"

"Yes," I replied untruthfully, anxious to impress him. As a matter of fact my grandmother had made it for me. I do knit myself, the plainest possible patterns so that I can read or watch television at the same time.

"It looks complicated," he said.

"Oh, it was quite easy," I said airily.

After we had walked for a bit we found a green paddock and sat down in it. Several wekas came out of the scrub. They are friendly, curious birds, often walking just ahead or just behind people as though eavesdropping.

The shoulderbag I had with me was the same one I had taken on the launch trip so I had the remains of my lunch with me, and we threw crumbs to the wekas. We kept quite still and they came very close to us, and ate the last of our food out of our hands. They are flightless birds, and too trusting.

"We could wring their necks if we wanted to," Zoltan said.

"I'll wring your neck if you do."

"Oh, I wouldn't hurt them, I like them." he said. "You know, you are the first girl with red hair I have ever known."

"I don't like it much. I tried to dye it a different colour once. I don't know what I did wrong. I managed to dye my hands, the wash-hand basin and the bathroom floor, but my hair finished up exactly the same colour."

He laughed, then he said, "Gilding the lily a bit, wasn't it?"

He began to lift little locks of my hair, which is shoulder length, into the air between his finger and thumb, working round from the back to the right side so that I had to turn to him. Those Californian lilac blue eyes were looking into mine at very, very close range. That was when he kissed me. The only sound I could hear was loud heart-beats.

After a moment he said, "What are you thinking about?"

"I was trying to decide whether that was your heart I could feel beating, or mine."

"You're not serious."

I put my hand on his chest. "It's quite a serious scientific problem."

"Haven't you ever heard of two hearts beating as one?" he asked, with a cheeky grin, putting his hand on my heart.

"Don't take any liberties," I said.

"I certainly won't do anything you don't want me to," he said.

At that moment the friendly American lady saw us from the track.

"Are you coming back — it's almost time for dinner?"

She stood there waving and waiting for us, a short, fat, friendly figure with many rings flashing on her fingers.

We stood up and went over to her. Binoculars in an embossed leather case hung around her neck. A keen birdwatcher, she spoke enthusiastically about the birds she had seen. She was not at all offended when Zoltan and I burst out laughing when she pronounced the Maori names all wrong in her American twang. Her name was Mrs Roberts and she came from Oklahoma.

Back at the hotel we all dispersed to get dressed for dinner. I was getting through my wardrobe at a great bat, and was wondering what else I could wear to fascinate Zoltan.

Just before I left Dunedin I had bought a Pierre Cardin lavender blouse of pure silk with grey buttons and two collars, one of grey and one of lavender. After a great deal of fossicking around the shops I had found a skirt that went well with it.

When I was finished dressing I stepped out on to the little balcony, idly watching the people dotted in little groups below me. My attention was caught by a red Falcon coming up the drive. It stopped outside the main doors almost directly below me.

Patrick Livingston and his two companions from Rata House got out of the car and began to take the luggage out of the boot. Almost immediately I saw Zoltan emerge from the hotel and hurry over to them. Even from where I was standing, above them and a little to the side, I could see that they were not having a very amicable conversation. I was just too far away to overhear what they were actually saying.

Finally, with obvious resentment, they put the luggage back in the boot, got into the car and drove off. I noticed that their luggage consisted of two red suitcases and a green one.

Instinctively I slipped back through the French window, and through a chink in the curtain watched Zoltan stand for a moment looking after the car as it drove away. Suddenly he looked anxiously up at my window, and seeing no-one, he strode back indoors.

When he tapped at my door ten minutes later wearing a light-weight charcoal coloured suit with a pink shirt and pink and charcoal tie I didn't have time to greet him before we heard a low wolf-whistle from Mrs Roberts. The whistle was for Zoltan. Certainly he looked the picture of sartorial elegance. Mrs Roberts was wearing a red dress which, though it must have set her back a few dollars, made her look dumpier than ever, and she had squeezed a couple more rings on her plump fingers. The heels of her shoes were so high she looked as though she was walking on her toes.

Placing herself between us, she slipped one arm through each of ours and announced, "Come on, I'll buy you a drink before dinner."

After our drink we invited Mrs Roberts to dine with us and she accepted very readily. As we went into the dining room, Mrs Roberts teetering between us, I wondered at Zoltan's not mentioning Patrick Livingston. Perhaps he didn't wish Mrs Roberts to know that he was a policeman. Perhaps he thought it wasn't worth mentioning, I decided. Then again, Mrs Roberts was hard to compete with. She was not short of conversation. She told us all about her son and daughter, both doctors, and her dead husband, in her loud, unselfconscious American voice.

She ate with voracious zeal, exclaiming over the food to us and the delighted waiter.

The only remark Zoltan addressed specifically to me was, "That's a nice blouse. Did you make it?"

Normally I am a very truthful person, but he seemed to have this thing about women who made their own clothes.

"Yes, I did," I replied, catching Mrs Roberts short, sharp look of complicity as I looked down at my plate.

Secretly I vowed that I would take lessons in dressmaking at the Polytech in the evenings as soon as I returned to Dunedin. That way the next time Zoltan asked me if I had made something myself I could honestly say that I had.

Afterwards, when we were having coffee in the lounge, Mrs Roberts said, "I'm going to the Forest Service lecture tonight. They are showing a film about red deer."

Very quickly Zoltan said, "Well, there's something I have to do. Perhaps you could take Giselle."

"Certainly," Mrs Roberts said, beaming.

This turn of events did not please me. For one thing I had been looking forward to spending the evening with Zoltan, and for another I didn't like the way they had arranged an outing for me as though I was a child who had to be left in someone's care.

However, Mrs Roberts was a kind and generous person and I was not going to offend her by arguing the point. I could hardly tag along with Zoltan, wherever he was going, when he hadn't asked me. It occurred to me that he might have tired of my company, but this was such a disagreeable thought that I refused to entertain it.

He said, "I might be too late back to see you tonight. I'll see you for breakfast though, O.K.?"

"If you like," I huffily replied.

He excused himself then and we both watched him leave the lounge and sprint athletically up the stairs, Mrs Roberts gaze only slightly less admiring than my own.

"He's so charming, your young man," she said, "and so handsome."

I should have explained, I suppose, that he was not "my young man" and that I had barely known him before yesterday, but a curious vanity prevented me. Part of his wonderful charisma must surround me if people thought he was mine. And if enough people thought he belonged to me, perhaps one day he would.

Mrs Roberts fetched a cashmere stole from upstairs and I a purple velvet blazer and we set off to the Forest Service rooms. All through the film and lecture, which Mrs Roberts watched avidly, I wondered what Zoltan was doing. I crushed all thoughts of his sneaking off to meet another girl.

Certainly there were plenty of pretty girls on the island, but he had not had the opportunity to meet them. If he were engaged on police work he was probably not at liberty to tell me, an acquaintance of two days, anything about it. These and similar thoughts went around in my head constantly until the lights went on.

Everyone stayed for tea and biscuits, then Mrs Roberts engaged the Forest Ranger in an interminable discussion until all the others had left.

We set off back to the hotel in darkness, she holding my arm and, as she was still wearing those silly too-high shoes, leaning her considerable weight against me. Certainly she was enjoying her holiday. She had found the lecture interesting, the Forest Ranger erudite, the home-made biscuits delicious.

It occurred to me unkindly that she may have talked her husband to death.

As soon as we got back to the hotel I excused myself and went upstairs. I heard voices coming from Zoltan's suite.

I had taken a tree tomato from a bowl downstairs. I rolled it to Zoltan's door and guiltily stopped and listened long enough to assure myself that none of the voices were female.

It was not very late but I undressed and got into bed. I fell asleep, blissfully conscious that Zoltan was only a few yards away and that I would be seeing him again in the morning.

It was light when I woke up and switched on the radio.

The weather forecaster confirmed that it was going to be another good day. Before going to bed the previous evening I had rinsed out the lavender blouse and it had drip-dried, so I teamed it up with a pair of shorts. It was only 7.15, too early for Zoltan to knock on my door, so I wandered restlessly about touching things, looking at myself in the mirror, and glancing at my watch every half minute or so.

I was pleased and thrilled when, at 7.20, there was a knock at the door. I skipped over and opened it. Immediately two people shoved their way in, kicking the door shut behind them. The man grabbed hold of me and spun me around. One arm was across my throat, and the other held my own arms behind my back. The girl stuffed a handkerchief in my mouth. She brandished a pistol in my face. The barrel of it wavered from one eye to the other. Then she got my cream Burberry coat from the wardrobe and cut slits on the insides of the pockets. They made me put the coat on, pushing my hands through the slits and tying them in front of me. Then they buttoned the coat and wrapped a scarf around my face covering my gagged mouth. The girl picked my shoulderbag up off the bed.

I recognised them as the man and the girl from Rata House.

They pushed me through to the bedroom, opened the window, and between them bustled me down the fire escape. Even if anyone had seen us, which they didn't, nobody would have thought much about it. Yesterday I had noticed children rushing up and down the fire escapes, and a young couple climbing up to talk to some friends on one of the balconies.

In a moment we were on the ground and they shoved me into the back of the red Falcon. The man got in beside me. The girl got into the driver's seat and instantly sped off.

After we had got out of the little township of Oban I indicated by much eye-rolling that the handkerchief was choking me. The man pulled it out of my mouth. He now had the gun which he jabbed into my side.

I had not attempted to speak but he said, "Bloody well shut up."

There were not many people about and few of those even glanced at us. It was that time of day when breakfast was uppermost in everyone's mind.

It was such a ghastly journey that I don't know how long it took. The rope was cutting into my wrists and the barrel of the gun was painful in my side. I stole one glance at the man, but he looked as vicious as a cornered rat, so I dared not look at him again. The girl continued driving wordlessly and with reckless speed, churning up a great deal of dust.

At last we stopped and got out and walked up a dirt track overhung with ferns to a small two-roomed bach hidden in the bush. The door of the bach opened as we approached. It was no surprise to see Patrick Livingston standing there.

"You got her then," he asked unnecessarily.

"No trouble," the other man said, quite proud of himself. "She was expecting Zoltan."

Patrick Livingston gave him a quick warning glance out of those awful steely eyes.

When we were all inside the bach he said to the others, "You might as well untie her — she can't run away."

They undid my Burberry and cut the rope from my wrists with a Swiss Army knife. I stood uncertainly in the middle of the room. It was a small room with two narrow bunks on either side. Against one wall was a grubby unvarnished table and several chairs. The remaining wall had a tiny coal stove with an enormous cast-iron kettle boiling on it.

They seemed, now that they had me, to be uncertain what to do with me.

"Have a seat," Patrick Livingston said.

"I've had no breakfast," I said.

"Tough bickies," the little, vicious man said.

"You can make us all breakfast," Patrick Livingston said. "Steve, get the food."

The little man obediently went out to the meat safe, returning with bacon, eggs, bread and dripping, which he dumped on the table. "Get on with it," he said to me.

I got on with it. There was a large cast iron frying pan and some cutlery and crockery in a cupboard next to the stove. Soon I had the bacon and eggs sizzling in the pan.

I set the table as calmly as I could while the little man called Steve kept his hand on the gun on the table and Patrick Livingston played absent-mindedly with the Swiss Army knife.

"If there's no toaster and no butter I'll do some fried bread," I said.

Patrick Livingston nodded. I made great quantities and kept it hot in the oven. I had deduced that Patrick Livingston was the kingpin so I served him first. Then the girl and then Steve.

"Pepper and salt," Patrick Livingston said to no one in particular.

"There's pepper and salt in the cupboard, Margaret," Steve said, to the girl.

"Let her get it," Margaret said.

We thus established a chain of command, first there was Patrick Livingston, then Steve, then Margaret, and now me.

It was quite eerie sitting there with my three kidnappers. They were so hungry and ate so much I began to think they might have captured me solely to make breakfast for them, and that if I washed and dried the dishes and wiped the bench properly they would set me free.

A few moments before I sat down I made a pot of tea, using very dusty tea that could have been left there since the Gold Rush. Margaret and Steve declined the tea with contemptuous waves of their hands, and drank beer instead, but Patrick Livingston and I consumed all the tea from the large enamel pot.

Conversation was a lost art to them. I wondered how they would have reacted to Mrs Roberts.

After the meal I did the dishes using hot water from the cast iron kettle which I refilled from a rain-barrel outside the bach, while Steve stood in the doorway pointing the gun at me as though he enjoyed it.

"We aren't going to hang around here all day are we?" Margaret asked, as soon as the last beer bottle was empty. She had a whining, nasal voice that went perfectly with her appearance.

"Christ, I hope not," Steve said, looking at Patrick Livingston with timorous defiance.

"Somebody should stay here," Patrick Livingston said.

"She can't find her way back from here," Steve said, afraid he would be the one left with the boring task of guarding me.

He pointed to the other room. "We can lock her in there. Take her shoes, take all her clothes. Then we can go to the pub."

"Alright," Patrick Livingston said.

"Take off your clothes," Steve ordered me, before Patrick could change his mind.

I stripped off to my bra and pants. "I'm not taking anything else off," I said.

Steve looked aggressive but Patrick Livingston said, "O.K., that'll do."

As he opened the door to the other room I picked up my shoulderbag from the back of my chair. Steve immediately grabbed it and rifled through it. It didn't contain much, just a comb, a handkerchief, a small make-up bag and a change-purse. He opened the purse.

"Christ, only five dollars," he said, but he took it just the same.

I picked up my shoulderbag from the floor where he had dropped it. He flung me into the other room and as I landed on one knee I heard the bolt rasp on the door behind me. Then they all ran like dogs off the leash to the car.

A small figure in a gorgeous fur coat regarded me from a tatty armchair as I straightened up.

"Mrs Livingston, I presume," I said.

5

Serrated Teeth

The old lady seemed to be as amazed at my style of dress as I was at hers. She stared at me for a considerable time, taking in my bikini briefs and half-cup bra with a scandalised air.

As for me, the idea of anyone wearing a fur-coat, however fabulous, on such a hot day, was astounding.

"Aren't you the girl with the dogs?" she asked me.

When I nodded, she asked me, "Who are those people?"

"Well, one of them is your grandson, Patrick Livingston. The other two are called Margaret and Steve."

"My grandson Patrick died when he was five years old — nearly twenty years ago."

I digested this. "Who is he, then?"

"An imposter, obviously."

"I can see that, but for what purpose?" I asked.

"I think they are bank-robbers," she said.

"But you don't have to change your name to rob a bank. If you get caught you go to prison whatever you happen to be calling yourself at the time," I pointed out.

"Well, they have robbed a bank. That's something I do know.

They have got a lot of money in that green suitcase. I heard them talking. They all have forged passports. They have just come from Australia."

"They may have just come from Australia, but they all have New Zealand accents," I said. "And I hardly think anyone would bother coming all the way from Australia just to rob a suburban bank in Dunedin of a few thousand dollars. There wouldn't be much profit after they'd paid their fares and split the proceeds of the robbery three ways."

"Perhaps they think it's better than working," she said.

"We've got to get out of here," I said.

We hadn't much hope of getting out. The room had one little window about two feet by one foot and it was covered with two layers of thick, closely woven wire mesh. I tried to pull at it with my fingers but I couldn't get any grip at all. It was held at the edges by lots of little horse-shoe shaped bolts.

I looked in my shoulderbag for my make-up purse, which contained amongst other things a nail-file, tweezers and nail scissors. I thought I might file through a few pieces of the mesh with the nail-file, but only the merest point of it would get through and that was the part with the plain steel.

After that I tried to pry the netting from the bolts, using each instrument in turn as my hands got sore holding on. After half an hour one tiny piece of wire had been worked free of the bolts. I rested my hands for a moment.

"You had better put some clothes on," Mrs Livingston said. "You look like a little tart dressed like that."

"I did have some clothes on when I came, you know. I don't go around in public dressed like this." I said irritably.

"There must be something the matter with you wearing things like that," she said.

She took off her fur coat. Underneath it she wore two jerseys and a cardigan. She took one of the jerseys and handed it to me. She was considerably smaller than me and I felt like a skinned rabbit in it. Then to my amazement she divested herself of a voluminous pair of bloomers and handed them to me also.

"Oh, Mrs Livingston, you can't go around with no pants on. What would people say!" I teased her.

"I always wear two pairs," she said. "And two vests."

I knew I looked highly comical in Mrs Livingston's gear, but it was worth it to take the look of righteous indignation off her face, and it was not as warm in the bach as it was outside in the sun. The part of the bach that we were in was overhung with trees, and no sunlight could penetrate.

I continued working on the wire-netting. Three hours and four broken fingernails later I had about six inches of mesh along the bottom of the window free and an equal amount up one side.

We were chatting intermittently.

"What I can't understand is your role in all this," she said.

I was a bit exasperated by this.

"My role in all this is that I tried to help you. I went to the police when I realised you had called for help."

"Well, that young man who came the day after the others arrived — the one who said he was a policeman, is that your boyfriend?"

"No, he is not. I just met him that day. And he *is* a policeman."

"Well, why didn't he arrest them? I told him they had burst into my house and that one of them was pretending to be my grandson. He told me I would be perfectly all right and they wouldn't harm me. He said they would be leaving in a few minutes. They didn't leave until the next day and of course as you can see, they brought me here with them."

It seemed incredible to me that Zoltan had left Mrs Livingston there with three bank-robbers, whatever promises he had extracted from them. And as Mrs Livingston had asked, why hadn't he arrested them? Even if he knew they were armed and he himself presumably was not, he had only to use his radio telephone to get reinforcements from the station.

"I think," Mrs Livingston said importantly, "that they would have killed me if it hadn't been for your friend."

"He is not my friend," I said. It was very deflating to realise that Zoltan had merely been paying me attention to lull any suspicions I might have had and to keep me out of their way. Now it was obvious that he was in cahoots with them. No wonder he had been furious when I arrived at Stewart Island, and he had seen me sitting drinking with the Captain. I continued angrily pulling the wire from the bolts with the nail-file.

"I think he's a bent cop," I said.

"A what?" She asked, mystified. I realised that she had probably never read anything later than Jane Austen or Anthony Trollope.

"A bent cop. A cop is a policeman..." I began.

"My dear child, I am not an idiot." Mrs Livingston said.

"Well in that case you know what bent means, too. It means crooked. He's a bent cop."

She thought this over. "It's very difficult to imagine," she said at length. "I couldn't help trusting him and he has such beautiful blue eyes, don't you think? Exactly the shade of my Californian lilac."

"I don't remember noticing that," I said, lifting my chin proudly to show my utter indifference. "And it doesn't seem to me to be very sensible to judge people's character by the colour of their eyes."

Her shrewd old eyes studied me as I went on picking bad-temperedly at the netting. I was faster at it now, having evolved a system of holding the bolt slightly out from the wood with the curve of the nail scissors and pulling the netting out with the tweezers or nail-file in my other hand.

Secretly I agreed with Mrs Livingston. I did not think that sincerity is something anyone can pretend to have.

But then again he had that curious habit of looking away, as on the occasion when I had asked if I could go to Rata House with him. And there was the evasive answer he had given Marilyn and Sally when they asked him if he was working or not.

Surely the police were entitled to a holiday in peace the same as everyone else.

At last I had pulled out enough of the wire-mesh to attempt to slip through the window. I had been standing working on the only chair. I thought of shoving Mrs Livingston through first somehow, but she was not agile enough and at her age she could easily break a hip or a leg dropping to the ground below, although it was no great distance.

However, she clambered up on to the chair and held the unpicked portion of the netting back for me in her claw-like, arthritic hands while I wormed my way through inch by inch. There wasn't time to make the hole in the window any bigger.

Our abductors could come back at any moment.

The drop from the window was only about nine feet, if that, but I had to fall out head first, grazing my knees on the window ledge in spite of Mrs Livingston's voluminous bloomers.

Luckily, I landed in some tree ferns.

I ran around to the single outside door of the bach, and looked around desperately for something to break the lock with.

There was nothing. There were a couple of dozen empty beer bottles piled up, quite expertly, to one side. How could I break the padlocked door with these? Then I realised the window in the other room was just glass, with no mesh. I heaved several bottles at it. The noise was terrible but there was nobody but us to hear. With one of the remaining bottles I crushed the little jagged pieces of glass at the lower edge of the window and climbed in. With the cast iron frying pan I broke the look of the door separating the two rooms, and Mrs Livingston emerged in her fur coat with the frightened haste of a small animal escaping from a trap.

As she came through the door looking small, frail and nervous I realised even more vividly what a responsibility and a hindrance she would be.

She had had nothing to eat or drink that morning. The kettle was boiling and I had noticed a thermos flask in one of the cupboards. While I ransacked the cupboards which contained only the remains of the bread and a tiny jar of marmite, she made some tea, which we poured almost immediately into the flask. I put this frugal repast into my shoulderbag. Previously I had always complained it was too big to look smart, but I was glad now that it was so capacious.

We were both edgily listening for any sign of the return of our captors. They had been away for hours and bored as they had all complained of being while watching us, they would have to come back sometime.

Quickly we left the bach. Neither of us had any idea where we were but I felt that as soon as we got to the dirt road we might recognise some landmark.

It was only seconds after closing the door that we heard the sound of a car. For a moment we clung together like Hansel and Gretel. Quickly I pushed Mrs Livingston into the forest, quietly exhorting her to run for her life. She did. It was incredible really how spry she suddenly became. I caught flashes of her skinny little legs under the long fur coat, and her stout old lady's shoes, as she tore ahead of me.

Soon I made her stop. Our headlong flight was not silent. Provided they did not see or hear us they would not know how long ago we had escaped, or where we were. While I peered through the bush, Mrs Livingston stood behind me, quivering with fear and exhaustion. We could not hear any voices but this did not surprise me. Steve, Patrick and Margaret, morose and silent by nature, spoke only when necessity demanded.

As my eyes became accustomed to squinting through the myriad leaves and branches I made out the figure of a lone man standing outside the bach. He was tall, fair and heavily built, and his face was as round as a tennis ball.

"Who is it?" Mrs Livingston squeaked.

"His name's Peter. He's a policeman."

"He isn't another bent cop, is he?" she asked.

"It wouldn't surprise me," I said.

So they were all in it together. No wonder he had feigned scepticism when I had spoken to him at the police station.

Zoltan had been cleverer, more subtle. He had thought I mightn't let the matter rest, and known I would, at the very least, call at Rata House on my way home to make sure Mrs Livingston was all right.

Now I said, "Look, he's puzzled. He might look around up here for a few minutes. Let's see if we can take his car."

Again we plunged through the bush only slightly compromising speed for silence. The birds were making a terrific din, but somehow Peter did not seem the person to notice if their noise was louder than usual. As I had hoped, he had left the keys in the car. We leapt in and I turned it quickly. The sound alerted him and we heard him tearing down the path. He reached us just as we sped off. I even heard him shout, "Wait. Stop, Stop. Don't go!"

We were congratulating ourselves on our escape. I was particularly worried about Mrs Livingston, hoping she wouldn't have a heart attack or a stroke or anything.

After I had been driving at top speed for about five minutes I saw a bend in the narrow road, so I slowed down. As we rounded the bend another car, coming from the opposite direction, appeared. It was a red Falcon. For a timeless, dreamlike moment we gazed into the astonished faces of Patrick, Steve and Margaret.

They didn't wait to turn their car. Patrick and Steve leapt out. They both had guns. I heard the shots. The glass of the rear window shattered. They were aiming for the tyres. Considering that they were both probably drunk they were quite good shots. The car began to wobble dangerously. Then it stalled. I hopped out and Mrs Livingston scrambled out after me without having to be told. I took her hand and once more we dived into the native bush in the general direction of the sea.

The bush was particularly thick but it seemed to hinder our pursuers more than it did us. At least we had the advantage of being sober. We could hear them crashing about, tripping over trailing branches. Dreadful obscenities filled the air, but as we hurried on they grew encouragingly fainter.

Suddenly we came to one of those miniscule beaches that

edge Stewart Island. There was a boat there with its prow in the water. It was not a boat I would have cared to have got into in ordinary circumstances. It looked as though it had been there since God was a boy, but Mrs Livingston hopped in and I pushed it off, got in quickly and started to row like mad.

We were a hundred yards out to sea before they arrived at the little beach. They fired a couple of shots at us, but they must have run out of ammunition or realised it was hopeless. It gave me great pleasure to see them gesticulating wildly as they receded in the distance.

I still wasn't clear where exactly we were. Vaguely I thought we would come upon a launch or a yacht and be taken on board and whisked to safety. It was wiser to keep a considerable distance from shore because I knew Patrick and Co. could be watching for us, waiting for us to land.

After a time Mrs Livingston broke the bread into great hunks and spread the Marmite with her fingers. We wolfed it down. Then we had a half a cup of tea from the large thermos. When we had made the tea I had pictured us drinking it in a pleasantly leisurely manner in a glade in the bush while we rested on the long trek back to Oban.

A small island lay ahead of us. My arms ached from rowing, and my behind was numb. My hands, which had previously had dozens of little cuts from the broken glass and wire mesh, now had enormous blisters. The island looked a haven to us at that moment. The sea seemed to be taking us towards it. Some dolphins followed us for a while, leaping and bounding and diving enchantingly.

"Aren't they lovely," I said.

"Shall we give them some bread?" she asked.

"No, we aren't out of the woods yet."

A little distance off I saw a large fin sticking out of the water. It was a shark. It would have been unkind and unnecessary to point out the shark to Mrs Livingston. She was looking very much the worse for wear. Her snowy hair was in great disarray, and the afternoon sun and salt air had burnt her fine, fair skin cruelly, criss-crossing the wrinkles. Even the wondrous fur coat looked sorry for itself, splashed with sea-water and with little twigs and berries caught in the button-holes and collar.

When we drew into a little inlet on the island I grabbed hold of an overhanging tussock and hauled myself ashore. The water was very deep as the island seemed to rise out of the water without benefit of beach or shingle. Mrs Livingston stepped shakily ashore, clutching my arms while I held the boat close to the shore. I moored the boat to a branch of a short and rather weather-beaten tree. We moved to slightly higher ground and sat down. Only a few crusts of bread and a thermos that was already a third empty stood between us and starvation. Still, at least we were free.

The old lady took off her halfslip, which was of white lawn. She probably considered nylon "tarty." She began tearing it into strips.

"What are you doing?" I asked.

"This is for you."

"Mrs Livingston, I am not about to go into labour."

"Don't be coarse," she said, a fiery look in her faded eyes. "I am going to bind up your hands."

Goodness knows what Girls Own Adventure story she had got that out of, or some tale of the Great War when she was in her youth.

She tottered down to the water's edge in her awful lace-up shoes with the thick high heels, that to her were a very modern derivation of elastic-sided boots. More to humour her than anything else I let her wrap my hands in the water soaked bandages.

"That salt water hurts like anything," I complained.

"It will help them to heal," she assured me.

We took turns watching for passing boats, she taking first watch while I lay down to rest. It was a worrying situation but Stewart Island was as full of boaties and fishermen as it was of campers and trampers. We would soon be picked up, with any luck before evening and certainly in the morning.

It was getting cooler and duller on the little island.

Mrs Livingston had spread her fur coat out to dry, flung over some bushes, and was wandering about, exclaiming about this or that plant or blossom, for all the world as though we were on a picnic.

"What are all these holes, these burrows?" she asked. "They're not rabbit holes."

"They are burrows," I said. "We're on a mutton-bird island."

Gradually the sound of a motor-boat impinged on our consciousness, the furtive throb coming over the water. Mrs Livingston waved her stick-like arms. I stood up and we both peered in the direction of the sound. Evidently Mrs Livingston was as short-sighted as I was. The boat was in quite close before we realised that the person standing on the bow of the boat was Margaret, and that she was pointing a gun, waveringly, at us.

Patrick was at the wheel, and Steve, now armed with a shotgun, was next to him. They seemed to have quite a little arsenal to choose from. They were full of murderous intent as they cut the engine and nosed in. There were not even any rocks of sufficient size close at hand to throw at them.

It had become second nature to me to grab my shoulderbag when we were in danger.

"Stay here and hide," I told Mrs Livingston, and she ducked down behind the foliage as I crept forward.

They drew in directly in line with the spot where they had just seen us, where the ground was higher than our own landing place.

Margaret had climbed over the guard in front of the steering wheel and was now crouching on the ship's pulpit. Looking slightly insane she called angrily, "Come on, you bitches, you're coming back!"

As she half rose from her crouch to grab at a fern I uncorked the thermos and tipped the hot tea over her upturned, hard young face. Reflexively she dropped the gun and screamed. Even her scream had a nasal quality. Her hands went immediately to her burnt face and she plopped in the water, thrown a few feet by the rocking of the boat. Steve fired one wild shot at me. More to get rid of it than anything else, I threw the empty thermos at him. To my great surprise it hit, just a glancing blow on his shoulder.

"I'll bloody kill you!" he bawled.

It became immediately obvious that Margaret couldn't swim. While she threshed about in the water in a state of panic Steve and Patrick hunted for a lifebelt, but they didn't have one on board. Neither of them could swim either, by the look of it, because they didn't jump in to help her. They just stood there futilely beckoning her in.

Perhaps I was the first one to see the shark. It flashed up so quickly, attracted by the splashing and squealing. Just below me, it happened. The shark's great maw opened and I registered that it was a white-pointer, because all its teeth were serrated.

I must have learnt that at school, and it came into my mind as I heard it crunch right through Margaret's arm near the shoulder. The water coloured with the most incredible amount of blood.

Apart from Patrick firing one shot, he and Steve acted with a total lack of heroism. They couldn't actually have done anything useful, but they turned the boat around with indecent haste and took off at top speed. The shark was about seventeen feet long, bigger than their boat.

Margaret sank briefly and came up again. The shark turned, and came in again swiftly, its fearful grey body flashing in the blue-green sea. Its merciless grey eyes looked into mine as its jaws closed again on Margaret. She was no longer conscious, she may not even have been alive. Certainly she had stopped screaming.

I backed off on my knees through the profusion of shrubs to where Mrs Livingston was cowering. "They've gone."

"Did that shark get her?" She asked.

So she had seen the shark from the rowing boat and not mentioned it.

"Did you know the white-pointer shark is the only kind whose teeth are all serrated?" I asked her.

"You'd better sit down," she said. "It's a pity you had to see it."

We had been quite cheerful really, before. Well, not cheerful, but optimistic and certain that we would shortly be rescued, and that nothing untoward would happen until then.

Mrs Livingston kept patting my hand and urging me to think of something else. The funny thing was that until the shark attacked her I had not considered Margaret to be a human being. Her part in the abduction of a frail old lady who could have died of shock at any moment had seemed so cruel and awful that I honestly felt that she and Patrick and Steve belonged to some different and alien species. For the first time it occurred to me that she probably had parents still living.

I didn't feel any guilt about her death. Certainly they would have killed us by now, but for some restraining factor unknown to us. Still, I felt a bundle of nerves. Although I knew it was impossible I nevertheless had visions of the shark flinging itself onto the island and grabbing me.

After sitting numbly for a time, we began pulling soft ferns and grasses together to make a bed for the night as it would soon be dusk. We lay down together in the gathering darkness covered by the fur coat. Knowing we had nothing to drink made us feel thirstier.

In order not to think of the dead Margaret we tried to puzzle out why I had been kidnapped. We had already come to the conclusion that Patrick would have released Mrs Livingston as soon as they made their getaway from Stewart Island. Surely being lumbered with a very old lady was a big enough nuisance without having to keep an eye on me, too.

As criminals go, they were not very bright. The fact that they were lugging the stolen money about with them in the same green suitcase they had originally stashed it in was tempting fate, even if there are plenty of green suitcases about.

Rather foolishly we had taken it for granted that we were now safe. It had not occurred to us that Patrick and Steve would come back. When we heard the motor we both jumped up, thinking we were about to be rescued. Just as I recognised Steve, a bullet whistled past my shoulder. As their boat neared the island the most enormous dark cloud appeared in the sky. It hovered over them, briefly, but it moved more quickly than they did. The mutton-birds were coming in for the night. They landed, hundreds at a time, either straight on to the island or on the water, walking on the water to the island. They screeched and yelled and bumped into each other and into us, scrambling into their burrows.

We heard the boat leaving again to the sound of much cursing. Steve and Patrick used such awful language and so continuously that it was funny, rather than shocking.

One might have thought that after a day at sea the mutton-birds would have settled down immediately, but they hopped about visiting each other. We kept very still and they clambered about us, quite indifferent to our presence. They may have thought we were a couple of boulders. Eventually we all slept peacefully, Mrs Livingston, the mutton-birds, and me.

6

In Spite of Respite

In the early morning the mutton-birds woke us with their cries, sounding like a lot of angry babies. Mrs Livingston was rather nervous of them, but they merely watched us curiously, their humble sweet faces turning this way and that as we got ready to leave.

Working on the principle that the sooner we left the sooner we would get something to eat and drink, we clambered into the boat almost before it was light. Caught in the tussock that hung into the sea was the lower part of a white and bloodless arm, the sight of which added great impetus to our departure.

Rowing was quite difficult with my blistered hands, so Mrs Livingston took one oar for a time, in spite of my protestations. Progress was slow, but at least we didn't see any more sharks. The waters of Foveaux Strait abound in them all year round, as the warm current from Australia that surrounds Stewart Island encourages them. It is said that sharks never sleep, but they must have all been sleeping that day.

After we had been rowing in our pitiful fashion for about an hour and a half we began to pass, or more correctly, *be* passed by other boats and small ships. On my previous visits to Stewart Island, Foveaux Strait had seemed thick with launches and yachts and runabouts. Now that we needed them they seemed very thin on the water. Those we did see either ignored us, or the occupants responded to our shouts and waves by shouting and waving cheerily back. From their point of view it was just an exchange of merry badinage. It was all very frustrating.

When I saw a keeler quite near us, with cerise sails and the name *Neptune's Daughter* in bold white letters I couldn't at first believe it. I didn't call out "Help," or "We're starving" or anything like that. Making a loud hailer of my hands, I called "David, David, David!" because they say nothing is as sweet to anyone as the sound of their own name, and I thought it the most likely word that he would hear. It worked. The keeler slowed down. David, replete with peaked cap and looking elegantly nautical stood staring at us. Christine and Tim were with him.

Mrs Livingston said, "I hope they are respectable."

She must have concluded I knew only bank-robbers and bent cops.

"They are my flatmates," I said, as though that was respectable enough for anyone.

With much difficulty they got us both on board and tied the faithful little rowing boat to the stern, already hoping we wouldn't be met by the irate owner. My friends immediately began to fall about laughing at my appearance, pointing out my bloomers and skin-tight cardigan to each other amid great explosions of mirth.

Eventually Christine cooked us bacon and eggs and we had lots of tea, while they explained they had all had a free weekend. Unable to make up their minds what to do and where to go they had decided they might as well sail the keeler down to Stewart Island to surprise me. It had taken them only thirty hours, quite good time.

When we told them the story of our kidnapping they were quite mystified.

"I can't understand their trailing you about with them," Tim said. "Only calling attention to themselves when you were both discovered missing."

"I doubt if anyone would have missed me," Mrs Livingston said. "I never go anywhere. If they had killed me in my own home it would have been days or even weeks before anyone found me. No-one will have noticed my absence from Rata House."

"I wonder if anyone's noticed my absence from the hotel," I said. "I suppose Mrs Roberts has. She's a chatty American guest at the hotel. I suppose she'll be bending someone else's ear by now."

"Why don't your friends all come and have lunch at your hotel with us?" Mrs Livingston said. "My shout."

There was much good-natured argument about whose "shout" it would be, but in the end they all agreed to come with us.

Christine lent me some jeans which fitted quite well when clasped with a belt round my waist, and the legs rolled up at the bottom, and she also unwillingly lent me a new white jersey which she had never worn.

At the hotel we got a table almost to ourselves. A courteous elderly American gentleman shared our table due to shortage of seating. He paid a lot of attention to Mrs Livingston and she got quite coy, behaving as though he was proposing marriage every time he passed her the salt or sugar.

Far from being shattered by all our recent exploits, she seemed to have taken a new lease on life and enjoyed the company of my flatmates who were friendly and considerate to her.

"What will you do now?" Tim asked. "Do you think you should come back with us?"

"Oh, I think I'm quite safe now. Patrick and Co. have probably cleared well away to Dunedin at the very least by now."

"I don't think you should stay here," Christine said.

"Mr Bennet will be pretty annoyed if I don't have a full report about Stewart Island when I go back," I said. "He likes to get value for his money."

"Well, at least go down to the local police station and report what's happened," Tim persisted.

"I had intended to do that anyway," I said.

When we had finished dinner we all sat out on the lawn in front of the hotel, the females on deck chairs and the men sprawled on the grass.

Tim and Christine and David had decided to go back to Dunedin as Christine would have to go back to work quite soon after they got home. They were about to leave, and I was about to see if Mrs Livingston could book in at the hotel, sharing with me if necessary, when Zoltan and Peter appeared on the drive.

They both quickened their pace when they saw me.

"What's been happening?" Zoltan enquired anxiously.

"As though you didn't know," I said.

"Well, I deduced that you'd been kidnapped. Then the others told me that they had you in that old bach. I sent Peter around to rescue you."

"How is it that you are so friendly with them?" I asked suspiciously.

"Come over here so that we can talk privately," he said, and with a great show of reluctance I went with him and Peter to the only patch of lawn not cluttered with sunburnt bodies.

"Why did they tell you where I was if you weren't in on that bank raid?"

"The bank raid is nothing. I knew nothing about it until after it happened. They did that out of boredom. We didn't haul them in because they are in the drug business. They think I'm a bent cop, which I daresay is what you think. I am supposed to let them, or rather their boss, know if the police get on to them. I have a meeting arranged down here at Stewart Island with one of the top drug dealers. So far he hasn't shown up. We think he might be a bit leary about the meeting now. Evidently he was pretty annoyed about the bank robbery, and about you and Mrs Livingston getting involved. He guessed it was Steve and Patrick.

"Why didn't you come to rescue me yourself?" I asked petulantly.

"I had to wait here for Mr X," he said. "Besides, Patrick and the others would have been suspicious if I had left the hotel. Mr X may be staying at the hotel for all I know."

"You mean you don't know who he is?" I asked. I laughed spitefully. "You actually call him Mr X."

"I don't know who he is or what he looks like. We have to call him something, you know. Can you swear your friends to silence? I've told Mrs Roberts that you had to dash off to visit a sick friend."

I stood there as sulky as a child, thoroughly narked that he had not seen fit to trust me with this information before, yet he wanted my co-operation now. He didn't trust me but I was supposed to trust him.

"Oh, very well," I said.

He looked very relieved. "I'll make it up to you, Giselle."

"That's all very well. I've had some very hair-raising experiences, you know. That Steve is trigger-happy — he kept pointing that pistol at me. They've got more weapons than the Israeli Army."

"He would never have killed you. He had orders not to harm you at least until he got here. Don't you see that killing you two would have called attention to Stewart Island?"

"Maybe so, but don't forget I saw that silly Margaret eaten by a shark about two feet from me. I'm liable to have nightmares about that for the rest of my life. How you could expose anyone to experiences like that I just don't know."

"You surely don't imagine that I knew they were going to kidnap you — or Mrs Livingston," he said, sounding genuinely aghast. "After I left Rata House that day I went back to report to my superior officer. He wasn't available. When I contacted him at last, they had already left with Mrs Livingston early the next day. Then when they arrived here, they told me that Steve had tried to push you off the *Wairua*. They came to the hotel the day before yesterday when you were in your suite. I told them to keep away from you, and that the Syndicate would not be pleased if they called attention to themselves, or me, or you. They promised me that they would just keep away from you and remain completely out of sight. They are really dumb. They are either drunk or on drugs most of the time. I think Mr X will give them the chop after this."

At that moment I heard a familiar American voice. Mrs Roberts had the elderly gentleman who had been at our table trapped by one of her unstoppable monologues. She was dressed in a bright red trouser-suit, so squat and square that she looked as though she had been driven into the ground. When she saw me, an expression of delight crossed her face and, waving furiously, she headed towards us like a pillar-box suddenly come to life.

Zoltan said hastily, "Remember, I told her you had a sick friend on Stewart Island you had gone to visit. Please don't tell her what really happened. You know she'll tell everyone without meaning to. We mustn't frighten Mr X off."

Mrs Roberts flung her arms around me just then. "How is your friend. Is she any better?"

"Yes, thanks, and it was great seeing her again," I said. "What have you been doing yourself?"

She told me in great detail everything she had done, thought, and eaten since I had last seen her. It was good to see her and hear her. She seemed such a nice, real, safe person.

"We're going now, Giselle," Christine called out to me, but without moving, so that I would have to introduce Zoltan to her.

"Who are those people?" Zoltan asked.

"They are friends — they are my flatmates. They rescued us when we escaped from the mutton-bird island this morning. And that's another thing," I said. "How would you like to sleep with a few thousand mutton-birds?"

He and Peter started to laugh, but it still wasn't very funny to me.

Zoltan said, "You won't mind if I come over and meet your friends?"

"Oh, do," I said. "I'm sure you'll do exactly as you please, regardless."

We joined the others and I made introductions all round. During the stroll down to the yacht David invited Zoltan and Peter on board for a drink. When they agreed, Christine said, "Be warned, he's like Idi Amin on the ship. Do this, don't touch this, keep out of the way."

David smiled broadly. As soon as we went on board, drinks were handed round. Zoltan admired the yacht and David said, "It's practically my home — the only thing of value I have in the world." He grinned at Christine. "That's why I behave like Idi Amin, or Captain Bligh as Giselle calls me."

I told them not to mention to anyone that Mrs Livingston and me were kidnapped. "The police don't want to make Mr X nervous."

"You mean you actually call someone Mr X?" David asked, laughing heartily.

Zoltan fixed him with a cool stare.

Those of us who were not sailing got off the boat. "When will you be coming back?" Christine called.

"A day or so, maybe three. I'll stay at Perkin's Hotel in Invercargill for a night anyway."

We didn't wait for them to set sail but went back to the hotel.

Peter walked behind with Mrs Livingston, his hand under her elbow. Poor old lady, she hadn't had so much attention for a long time.

Zoltan said, "By the way, I've got some of your clothes."

"What clothes?"

"Oh, you know, your shorts and that lavender blouse you and Pierre Cardin ran up between you."

I got quite red and embarrassed. "I was trying to impress you, then."

"And now?" He asked.

"I may not bother any more."

"Didn't it occur to you that I was impressed already without your having to pretend you were the world's greatest dress-maker?"

"What I think," I said slowly, "is that you were paying me a lot of attention to keep me occupied so that I wouldn't spoil your plans. I think you are after a quick promotion."

"And if I am?" He asked. "I'm also trying to bust a very highly organised drug-ring that is going to cost a lot of New Zealanders their lives if I don't stop them."

"How very fortunate we all are to have someone like you on our planet," I said.

"O.K.," he said, trying to sound airy but looking very wounded. "I shouldn't have made a speech. Look, you may think you've seen some bad things these last two days, and met some lousy people, but I've seen worse and met lousier. Still, I know how you must feel. I intended to protect you and I made a mess of it. Nothing would have induced me to knowingly put you and Mrs Livingston in danger. But if you won't believe what I'm saying now, how come you're so sure you would have believed me before? Supposing I had broken all the rules and told you what I was doing here; supposing I had told you that Patrick and Steve were pushers; that I was pretending to be bent so that I could meet Mr X and get enough evidence to put him away… You'd have believed me then, would you?"

I stopped and looked full at him. "A couple of days ago," I said, "I would have believed anything you told me."

We walked on, both bristling, neither of us certain what the other felt.

Back at the hotel Mrs Livingston and I made straight for our suite. The management were quite agreeable to her sharing with me. I told her what Zoltan had said.

"The trouble is we don't really know if he's bent or pretending to be. Do you think we should go and see the Stewart Island policemen?" Mrs Livingston asked.

"There is only one," I said. "We'll sneak off and tell him — just to be on the safe side."

We crept down the fire escape, or rather I did. Mrs Livingston clattered down behind me in her awful shoes. She made no complaint. She was becoming addicted to adventure.

The Stewart Island Police Station consists of a tiny little lock-up room in the grounds of the resident policeman's house.

As I'd seen it before, I knew where to go. There was no-one about and no-one answered the door, so we hung about uncertainly at the bottom of the path. Unbelievably the red Falcon appeared and Patrick and Steve got out, armed to the teeth as usual.

They held the back door open, wordlessly, waving us menacingly into the back seat of the car. Patrick got in beside us and Steve drove.

"Get down, put your heads down or I'll blow them off," he said.

We put our heads down and nobody spoke until we stopped about ten minutes later.

"Get out," Patrick ordered, and we got out, all cramped and stiff-necked.

They had a helicopter hidden in a field surrounded by young trees. We scrambled into the helicopter and took off with Patrick at the controls. He flew low to begin with, stealthily, taking a westerly course to avoid being seen crossing the water off Paterson Inlet, then tacked off to the South East. Patrick's flying was erratic, not always intentionally so. We sped over the high bush, with Totai Flat chillingly visible in the distance.

Just as we landed on a little beach I recognised Tia Island out of the corner of my eye. We were at Port Adventure. It wasn't much help to know that, except it lifted my morale slightly to at least know where I was, because we were bundled out of the helicopter and taken to a church in the little inlet called Abraham's Bosom. The church was tiny, just one room. Only its minute steeple differentiated it from a bach. That, and a bell with a rotting rope.

Steve guarded us like a vicious dog, watching every movement. I overheard them discussing whether to tie us up, but, incompetent as ever, they had no string. They finished up deciding to watch us constantly. The chances of our escaping from here were very slender even without their constant surveillance.

At least we couldn't blame Zoltan this time. He hadn't even known that we were going to visit the Stewart Island Police Station. Zoltan had said that the drug-dealers had resources I wouldn't dream about. Maybe they had, but they were not very good on the accommodation side. The little church was even barer and more primitive than the bach. There were two rickety pews which Steve and Patrick made it clear they intended to keep for themselves while we cringed in a corner.

We were certain the police would begin to look for us fairly soon. Zoltan and Peter would notice our absence quickly, and I had made a vague arrangement to see Mrs Roberts in the dining room. Zoltan would no doubt tell her that I had dashed off to see another sick friend, not caring that she must think me impulsive and unreliable, besides having an extraordinary number of broken reeds amongst my acquaintanceship.

A lot of fit looking young men had been lounging about in the hotel dining room who hadn't been there the day before. The island must have been crawling with cops. The only question was, would we really be safe until they found us?

The duty of a prisoner of war is to try to escape. We exaggerated our cringing to satisfy the sadistic nature of our captors. When the beer came out, our chance would come. It was a shock to discover they had none, for they would not be quiescent for long without it.

Patrick came in with a dusty tin. "Look what I've found," he said.

Steve grinned. They held out the tin so we could see its contents. It contained a red katipo, New Zealand's only poisonous spider.

We were frightened then. We didn't have to pretend any longer. They transferred it, with due respect, to a glass jar. All of us watched it with horrid fascination. Mostly it remained very still, even though Steve tormented it at intervals by tapping the glass jar with a grubby finger.

This was their only entertainment, and they could very easily tire of it. Fear of incurring Steve's unpredictable malice kept us silent. Of course, he would hardly allow the katipo to bite one of us. He was supposed to keep us alive, and besides, it might bite *him*. He probably imagined that its poison is lethal, which is only rarely the case. Still, I knew it could make one very ill, causing acute abdominal pain and a kind of paralysis. And we were hardly handy to a hospital.

Steve kept staring at the katipo. At last he had met something more horrible than himself. Every now and then he shook the jar furiously either to assure himself that it was still alive, or to torment it. It clung to the glass in its still, spidery way and eventually he wearied of it, leaving it near him and glancing at it occasionally.

The one-roomed church was very cold. Pointing to the bell rope hanging down through a trap-door in the ceiling, I whispered to Mrs Livingston, "We can always hang ourselves if things get too bad."

She pursed her lips to show she wasn't amused, saying, "We've beaten them before. We'll do it again. They are two stupid men, and we are two intelligent women."

No use pointing out that there would be no boats left around this time. They were blocking all avenues of escape, and Mrs Livingston's brave sentiments didn't alter that.

With a magnanimity unusual in her, Christine had allowed me to keep the jeans and white sweater until I got back to Dunedin. Done no doubt to impress Zoltan and Peter. She had seemed to be quite taken with them, behaving with a lumbering coquetry towards them on the yacht, like an elephant hypnotised into thinking it is a kitten. The thought of how grubby and stained it was getting and her resultant rage cheered me up for a few minutes.

Two hours and a numb backside later we heard the chug of a motorboat.

"The cavalry's on its way," I said to Patrick.

"That's where you're mistaken," he said nastily.

"They're our friends, not yours," and he and Steve left the church with swaggering confidence.

We waited for them to come back. After a quarter of an hour I screwed up all my courage, opened the church door and peered out.

"You wait here," I said. "I'll see what's happening."

"I think I'd rather come with you," Mrs Livingston said.

"They may be giving us a chance to escape just so they have

an excuse to shoot us," I said. "You stay here."

I crept through the bush and down to the sea. There was no motorboat to be seen, but lying on the beach, each with a neat little bullet hole in the side of the head, were Patrick and Steve. The katipo was still in the jar. Very, very carefully, with my handkerchief over the lid, I set it free.

When I returned to the church, Mrs Livingston was peering out the window.

"Steve and Patrick have been shot. Some friends they had! Hurry up, we'd better move."

She appeared then at the doorway, blinking hesitantly at the sunlight, for all the world like Dreyfus set free after five years on Devil's Island.

"Are you sure it's safe?"

"It's safer out there in the bush than cornered in that little church."

That flushed her out immediately, and we navigated our way down the tracks to the beach.

As we had known intuitively, there were no stray row-boats lying fortuitously around Port Adventure, though we looked about all the same.

After a repetitious and pointless debate about whether the police would be able to guess where we were, we decided to try to fly the helicopter back.

"Are you sure you know how to operate it?" Mrs Livingston enquired dubiously.

"Oh, yes, we've got one on the farm," I told her with false heartiness.

"Perhaps we should wait for the police," she said.

"I'm sure someone must have seen or heard the helicopter leaving, but even if they tell the police it will be hard for them to find us. Anyway, we aren't safe here. We don't know who killed Steve and Patrick or why. They may come back for us. On the other hand they may not have known we were here. The sooner we are out of here the better."

That made her think again. We scrambled into the helicopter. Under her doubtful gaze, and after a great deal of tinkering, I got it into the air and we were off. I flew low over the tops of the trees. The nearer we were to the ground the safer I felt.

"Who could have killed them?" She asked.

"They are drug-pushers," I said. "They don't have a very long life-expectancy."

"Drug-pushers," she said, as though it was a foreign word.

"Yes, Zoltan is supposed to be meeting with the head man down here at Stewart Island. They call him Mr X. Steve and Patrick had turned into a couple of nuisances, what with robbing the bank and complicating matters by involving us."

"Mr X," she scoffed, unexpectedly. "You don't mean the police actually call him that."

"They have to call him something, Mrs Livingston," I replied, sententiously.

The engine began to falter. The fuel gauge was registering zero. "Hang on to your hat, I'm going to try to land."

We plunged on a horizontal course through the trees, chopping off large branches as we went. We would have been killed if we had hit the ground, but we landed on some half-grown trees, crushing them, settling quite nicely several feet above the earth. We couldn't get the door open, but it didn't matter, because the unbreakable glass was broken and we scrambled out on to a tiny patch of undergrowth in no time.

"I knew we should have stayed at Port Adventure," Mrs Livingston said maddeningly.

"Oh, shut up."

She looked quite crestfallen, "I'm sorry," she said. "You couldn't have known they wouldn't have filled the fuel tank."

"Wasn't it inconsiderate of them!" I said, and we both laughed.

Although neither of us was seriously hurt we were both covered in little cuts and bruises.

"Let's light a fire," she suggested.

"The Forest Service *would* be pleased, but the wrong people may see it. We aren't far from Port Adventure. We'll stay here for the night and head back there in the morning."

We sat and talked. Mrs Livingston spoke of her dead husband. He had died when she was thirty. When I asked her if she still missed him she astounded me, and herself I think, by replying, "I don't remember him."

They had had four children: two boys and two girls who had all predeceased her. I thought at first they must have died young or been cut off in their prime, and was surprised to learn that they had all lived sixty years or more.

No wonder she had stood up to all the recent hazards so well. You could end up with a fine disregard for all sorts of hazards after all that sorrow.

As night began to fall we went through the routine of gathering up leaves and twigs to sleep on.

"We must just about be qualified for our Queen's Scout badges by now." I said.

"I wish we had stayed at Port Adventure," Mrs Livingston said. "It's quite spooky here."

We lay side by side listening to the noises of the bush.

I hoped there weren't any rats around. There was nothing else in the bush to be afraid of.

"Why did you leave home?" Mrs Livingston asked me. "How

do you get on with your family?"

"The last person who asked me that was Zoltan. I get on very well with my family. As a matter of fact I took my friend Rona home with me for the weekend one time and she didn't believe we were real. She said we were like one of those families on television, all concerned about each other. The funny thing is, I went to her place for dinner one night and I thought they were like people out of a book, all arguing bitterly all the time. I thought it made her more interesting somehow. They all kept giving each other long, meaningful, bitter looks like people out of a Russian play."

"It sounds as though she is the one who should be living away from home." she said, adding after a pause, "I thought Zoltan seemed pleased to see you. How do you feel about him?"

"Well," I answered, suddenly embarrassed. "Since I am speaking in theatrical terms, one way of putting it is that before I met him my life was like black and white television, and after I met him my life was like colour television."

"In that case, let's hope he isn't too annoyed with us for sneaking off and getting captured again."

"Don't speak of it," I said. "Let's get some sleep."

7

Two Short Policemen

When morning came we were starving. We began plodding back to Port Adventure. Neither of us had much sense of direction, so it was just as well the police sent out a helicopter with a heat sensor attached to it. It was supposed to find us by our body heat. Last night Mrs Livingston had given off as much warmth as a skeleton, so I take the credit for the fact that they found us.

When we heard the helicopter and they saw us we went to a high clearing, shouting and waving. The helicopter landed vertically and two grumpy police pilots took us back to Half-Moon Bay.

The older and grumpier of them took us to the tiny police station at Half-moon Bay where Peter was waiting for us. Zoltan was not with him. When the local police constable had satisfied himself that we were physically all right, Peter drove us back to the hotel and we headed straight upstairs.

Zoltan came up to see us immediately. Mrs Livingston was in the bath and I was messing about making a pot of tea when he came in. We stared at each other. He was paler than usual, whether with anger or alarm I could not tell.

"I suppose you know you could have got killed," he said.

"I think I know that," I said.

"I thought I asked you to stay in the hotel?"

On hearing his voice, Mrs Livingston came into the room looking like Wee Willie Winkie, wearing my dressing gown, which was too big for her and trailed on the floor after her. Her pink scalp showed through her wet hair. She looked at least two hundred years old.

"It was all my fault, Senior Sergeant Baker," she said. "I insisted on going to the Stewart Island police. Giselle didn't want to go."

Zoltan was too well brought up to call an old lady a liar. After a moment during which he seethed with rage, he went over and put his arm around her, escorted her to the heater and switched it on.

"Don't catch cold, Mrs Livingston," he said.

"What happens now?" I asked.

"Peter and some of the others are going to Port Adventure to pick up the bodies. We have to keep all this out of the papers in the meantime. We'd appreciate it if you two ladies would say absolutely nothing to anyone for now. It would be nice if you co-operated fully for a change."

We two ladies hung our heads like a couple of kids.

"What I want you to do is stay here in your suite. If you aren't seen I may still be able to meet Mr X. It's possible he thinks you are dead or still lost in the bush. It's also possible that he himself is staying in this hotel, maybe he doesn't even know what you look like. I'm still waiting to hear from him. We will sneak you out at a quiet time, during the night if possible. Have you anyone you can stay with somewhere, Mrs Livingston?"

Rather sadly, she shook her head.

"Never mind, we can fix you up somewhere," he said.

"What about you, Giselle?"

"Oh, I must get back to work. I'll be alright if I can just get back to the South Island."

"You are causing a lot of trouble," Zoltan said. "You might get caught again. Either stay here, well out of the way, and have all your meals sent up or else go home to the farm. Or if you've got any friends who live in isolated places you could go and stay with them."

"The person who is causing the trouble is Mr X. If you were a cop's bootlace you would have caught him by now."

"I would have done if I hadn't half my mind on you."

He left then, giving me an aggrieved look from the door.

"I'm not going to be all cooped up in here," I said to Mrs Livingston.

"I do think we should do as he says."

"Why? What does he know. I'm getting the plane to Invercargill this afternoon. I'm fed up. You can stay here or go to a safe house or whatever you like."

"You don't suppose he could lock you up — just for your own good?"

"I shouldn't think so. It must be just like a doctor trying to operate on you for your own good — they can't do it without your consent."

Still, we did decide to have our lunch sent up. My suitcase was packed and I intended to sneak out somehow.

Zoltan came back in, looking so uncomfortable I knew he was going to apologise. But his eye fell on the suitcase.

"Right," he said through clenched teeth, "I'll fix you."

While I watched in outrage, he took my money, my cheque

book and my bankcard from my purse and pocketed the lot.

"You can't do that," I said, putting one hand on my hip. "I have certain rights."

"You do not have the right to mess up an important operation and you do not have the right to get yourself killed."

"Fascist pig," I yelled.

He stalked out without so much as a backward glance.

"He seems to have fixed you," Mrs Livingston remarked with an irritating note of admiration in her voice.

"That's what *you* think."

"Why, what can you do?"

"Plenty," I said, full of braggadocio. In fact it took me about half an hour to decide what to do.

After a frantic search in my handbag I picked up the phone. By a stroke of luck the captain of the *Wairua* was at his home and answered immediately. When I identified myself, rather diffidently, he seemed pleased but amused to hear from me.

"Do you remember you said I could ring you if I needed any help?"

"Of course. What can I do for you?"

"Could I get a lift on the *Wairua*, you know, without paying. I'll send you the money as soon as I get to Dunedin."

"Oh, don't worry about it. It'll be my pleasure."

"There's one other thing."

"Name it," he said. I was starting to think that he was absolutely adorable.

"You couldn't pick me up outside the hotel could you? At precisely 2 p.m.. Just draw up outside the front entrance and I'll come straight out. Don't ask for me at the desk."

After a few seconds pause he said, "O.K.. How's your boyfriend?"

"Which boyfriend?"

"You know the one I mean — the cop."

"I've had a row with him."

If he wanted to think I was leaving because Zoltan and I had quarrelled, it suited me. It would save a lot of explaining.

"Well, I'll call for you at two o'clock, then," and he hung up.

When it came time to leave I managed to alter my appearance somewhat by doing my hair differently, tying a scarf around my head low down on my forehead and wearing sunglasses. I was quite pleased with my ingenuity until the captain of the *Wairua* recognised me the moment I made my furtive exit from the hotel. When he opened the car door I hopped in smartly and he drove off like a get-away man at a robbery.

Within minutes of boarding we moved off. The captain spent part of the journey in the cabin with me and why not — it was his cabin.

"Do you need any money?" he asked.

"Well, could you lend me a few dollars for the bus to Invercargill?"

"What happens when you get to Invercargill?" he asked.

"I'll stay at Perkins Hotel. They know me. It's a cheap place I've often stayed at. My father can pay my account when he picks me up in the morning. I'm going to spend tomorrow at Mataura." I said.

He gave me some money, about fifty dollars.

"You know, you sure are a good friend," I told him.

"It's no trouble," he said.

Green about the gills but otherwise all right, I finally lurched off the *Wairua*, got the bus from Bluff and headed for Inver-cargill.

When I arrived in Invercargill I went straight to my hotel. I telephoned collect from the lobby and arranged for my father and Alistair to pick me up the next day. There was a creaky old-fashioned lift but I took the stairs to my room. It was a far cry from my suite at Rakiura. There was just a bed, a chair, a dressing table and a wardrobe stuck diagonally across one corner. I went to see a film I had missed when it was in Dunedin, had dinner and went to bed.

In the morning when a knock sounded on the door I thought it was a housemaid. When I opened the door two men were standing and smiling at me. They were both short and in their middle forties. One produced an I.D. Card showing that he was Inspector Bracken of the Invercargill Police. The other man was a sergeant. I didn't catch his name but I thought it was Simpson.

"We have instructions to ask you to come down to the station. There might be some information you can give us."

"Well, what is it you want to know?" I asked.

"Some of our chaps from the Drug Squad are there at the moment. They just want you to clarify a few points."

"But I'm waiting for my father and brother. They'll be here in half an hour."

"Don't worry," Inspector Bracken said. "We'll get you back in time."

I knew that they were not policemen. For one thing they were too short ever to have been accepted into the police force, especially at the time they would have been recruited. I remembered my father once telling me that twenty years ago, the height requirement had been six feet for the police.

By this time I was quite an accomplished kidnappee. I took a jar of make-up out of my suitcase and pretended to be concerned with my appearance while they watched, with expressions of amused tolerance. Instead of putting the make-up jar back into my suitcase I slipped it into my shoulderbag.

"Will I do?" I asked.

"You look very nice," they murmured in chorus.

We took the lift to the ground floor. None of us spoke, but whenever I looked at either of them they smiled at me without showing their teeth, in what was intended to be a reassuring way.

As we stepped out of the lift, I took the jar of make-up out of my shoulderbag just before I passed the fire alarm. Before they could stop me I broke the glass and pushed the button. Those awfully loud, jarring fire alarm bells sounded very sweet to me for once.

The hotel had been like a morgue a moment before, but suddenly people began rushing about all over the place. A crowd gathered from nowhere, some immediately outside the hotel and some across the street. The fire brigade arrived in seconds. A passing police patrol car drew up.

By this time I was mingling in the crowd, peeking at intervals between two tall bystanders. The two phony policemen were looking around them, as bewildered as everyone else.

I ran over to the patrol car and explained, not very coherently, what had happened. As soon as I said the word "drugs" the two policemen leapt out of their car. The two little men began, rather belatedly, to run up the street.

The crowds hampered them, at first accidentally, and then realising the police were after them, closed in and stopped them.

Inspector Bracken and Sergeant Simpson and I were all taken to the police station where telephone calls were made to Stewart Island and Dunedin.

The real inspector at the Invercargill Police Station seemed loathe to let me go. He seemed to think I should wait for Zoltan or get someone else to escort me back to Dunedin or Mataura, or wherever I was going. I explained that my father and brother were picking me up at the hotel, and that if my father heard of all my adventures over the last few days he would bring pressure to bear to make me go back home permanently. Of course we both knew I was too old to be forced to do this, but he agreed it would create a lot of unnecessary worry and bad feeling. I also said my father and brother and even I, myself, were handy with guns.

Reluctantly he let me go and I went back to the hotel in a police car, feeling very important. I apologised to the manager of the hotel, who was very affable and understanding. The police had already given him some kind of explanation about the false alarm and he was so pleased that his hotel hadn't actually been on fire he was ready to forgive everyone anything.

By the time my menfolk arrived all the excitement had died down. I checked out of the hotel quickly, so that no-one could mention to my father anything about the two men who had tried to abduct me, if anyone knew of it.

"How did you fill in your time waiting for us?" My father asked as we set off for home.

"Oh, I went to the pictures yesterday afternoon."

"So long as you weren't too bored," he said.

As soon as I could, I got Alistair on his own and told him all about it. Just showing off, really. His chief reaction seemed to be one of surprise that all these things had happened to me. It was quite easy to swear him to secrecy. For one thing he was taken up with his own interests so much that he would probably forget what I had told him without me there to remind him, and for another he had confided various matters to me over the years that he did not wish our parents to know about.

Fortunately my mother was preparing for a visit from both sets of grandparents, and was frantically baking and pickling and airing beds and generally going to all the needless trouble she went to when she was having people to stay.

After prolonged goodbyes the following morning, I left them at about 9 a.m. in my little Fiat.

8

A Good Reason to Knock

After an uneventful journey I got back to Dunedin about mid-day. It seemed like a good idea to go to the house to freshen up, and say a quick "hullo" to Frey and Charlie and The Cat before going to work.

As Huia Avenue is a blind street many people who don't live there park their cars in it, so for this reason I usually park near the corner. But today after I got out of my car I noticed there were no others about. Except for an elderly retired couple everyone in our street works, though some of them only part-time.

Ridiculous as it sounds, whenever I get back from being away I always sneak in, hoping to surprise The Cat into betraying some sign of affection at my sudden return, before he has time to compose himself into his attitude of total indifference.

After quietly turning my key in the lock I slipped into the hall. The Cat was on the window-seat in the lounge. I crept up, stroked his head and whispered, "Hullo puss." His only reaction was to look faintly irritated. Considering I had stopped off at the butcher in town specially to get him some fresh, topside steak, and having had to drive round and round several blocks to get a park and then walk quite a distance to the shop, I was disappointed. Still, I stayed patting him and murmuring to him for a few minutes.

A movement in the next room surprised me. David's room was next to the lounge. Grateful that he was there and bursting to tell him of the events he had missed, I hurried to his room. In my excitement and pleasure I forgot to knock at his door. All of us had been very strict about that — respecting each other's privacy and all that.

David was packing, but he wasn't packing clothes. There were a lot of little packets containing white powder, some on the floor and some in the suitcase. If it hadn't been for my recent experiences I probably would have thought they were little bags of sugar.

He went very white, and I went very white. We stared at each other.

"You have found out my little secret," he said, at last. "I wasn't expecting you."

"Evidently." I answered. He stared at me with an expression I could not read, saying nothing. "You're Mr X. You were joking about it, and it was you all the time."

"What else could one do but joke about it," he laughed. "In any case, I'm not Mr X, I'm not that important. Mr V maybe, or even Mr W, but not Mr X, not yet."

"You sent those awful men to the hotel."

"You mean they saw you? I thought they must have missed you. What happened to them? Don't tell me they bungled it."

"I knew straight away they weren't policemen."

"They didn't try *that?* They didn't pretend they were the *police!*" He was exasperated, a man surrounded by fools.

"They had phoney I.D.s, but they were so short I was suspicious of them immediately. And they didn't look any more like the police than The Cat does. They've been arrested. They'll tell Zoltan who you are."

"They don't know who I am. You're the only one who knows who I am," he said, a look of regret in his mild grey eyes.

"I'm not going to be kidnapped again, am I? It's getting a bit tedious."

"There isn't time for that," he said, "Besides, you know who I am now. Kidnapping won't be quite enough this time."

He sounded like a cowboy faced with the necessity of putting down a favourite horse. Once again I found myself staring into the barrel of a gun.

"David, you couldn't let me go, just for old times sake, could you?" I asked, my voice quavering a bit.

"If only you'd knocked on my door before you came in just now. I would have been able to get away without harming you."

"It just shows you how important good manners are, doesn't it?"

"It does indeed." David said.

While we had been talking I had been taking little involuntary steps backwards out of his room until I was standing in the passage, and he, equally imperceptibly, had moved after me.

Rather urbanely he stood in his doorway, saying, "You won't try to run away will you, Giselle?"

"Not while you're pointing the gun at me."

I strove to keep him talking. "How could you have killed Steve and Patrick?"

"I had nothing to do with that," he said, virtuously. "And why should I care if they are dead. They nearly messed everything up. I've never even met them, in any case. I've spoken to them on the phone a few times and that's all."

"Why are you in this business?" I was curious, and also desperately hoping that Tim or Christine would come breezing in.

"For the money, Giselle, for the money."

"But what good does it do you? I mean living in this house, with us, it's hardly palatial."

"True, but it's only for a short time. And I'm not often here. You should see where I stay sometimes. Besides, it provided me with an excellent cover, really. I mean, I was hardly calling attention to myself, was I? Sharing the rent with three others, living in an ordinary bungalow in a street where everybody's too busy to pry. And you and Christine, such nice respectable girls going about saying what a wonderful chap I am."

"But you could have been nice — you were nice — and you could have succeeded at something honest. I mean, you're clever and you've been quite lucky, your father left you that yacht."

He laughed. "My father didn't leave me that yacht. I bought it myself. I just told you that story. I knew I could rely on you to spread it around."

"As a matter of fact," I said, very offended, "I didn't spread it around at all, not until I realised that you seemed to tell everyone yourself anyway."

We heard The Cat jump to the floor, and watched as he left the lounge and stood waiting, very grandly, for one of us to let him out to the front garden. David, out of force of habit went immediately to open the door for him. With the gun still trained lazily on me, he felt for the door handle, turned it and opened the door.

Immediately Zoltan and Peter stepped into the passageway

and disarmed him. Through the open door I could see several armed policemen. The Armed Offenders Squad were staked out all over Huia Avenue, in the bushes, in the garden, and all around our house.

"Is anyone else here?" Zoltan asked me.

"Not as far as I know, I don't think so."

At a signal from Zoltan several policemen rushed in, and very quickly and quietly searched all the rooms.

One of them called to Zoltan, "It's quite a haul."

Practically everyone trooped down to David's bedroom then. Someone had handcuffed David and now pushed him along the corridor.

David said to Zoltan, "Inspired guesswork, was it?"

"Only partly. We got the shipping report in. I noticed that there was a yacht with your number and your colours off the coast of Oamaru on Saturday. We're always interested if a yacht's in two places at once."

"What do you mean?" I asked.

Zoltan said, "He owns two identical yachts. One brings the drugs into our waters, and the other sails out to meet it as though going for a little pleasure trip, and the drugs are transferred without the harbour police being suspicious about it."

He turned to David. "I'll get someone to take you to the station now."

"I'm all yours." David said. Then he turned to me, smiling, "Bye bye, Giselle. It was a privilege knowing you."

Other policemen besides Zoltan stayed, a police photographer and fingerprint man, and others who packed the heroin up and took it out to one of their cars. Peter spent a lot of time poking about outside the house, peering into sheds and corners, and a dog-handler arrived and he and his dog traipsed all over the place while The Cat glared at them from the gate-post. Zoltan followed me to the kitchen, and sat down on one of the straight-backed chairs.

"I'm making lunch. Mushrooms and bacon, do you want some?" I asked.

"Thank you. It sounds good."

The Cat came back in, and stood watching us, while I chopped up his steak.

"What a pretty cat," Zoltan said. "Hullo, puss."

The Cat jumped onto his knee, purring loudly. It was the first time I had ever heard that overfed alley cat purr.

"What's his name?" Zoltan asked, tickling The Cat under the chin.

"Judas, we call him Judas."

"Judas," he laughed. "That isn't a very nice name for you, is it, puss?"

The Cat treaded with his paws on Zoltan's lap.

"He'll miss David," I said spitefully. "He's no judge of character, that cat."

There was a sharp tap at the kitchen door and another policeman walked in. A very important policeman, I think he was the assistant commissioner. He introduced himself as Michael Lockwood. It was clear from the way he said his name that he thought everyone should already know who he was. Zoltan rose hastily when Lockwood entered, putting The Cat on the chair behind him.

"Miss Dougal," The Very Important Policeman said. "I think it would be a good idea if you went to stay with friends for a while. Preferably out of Dunedin."

Most people would have called him handsome, but hard-looking. His jaw was as square and determined as any comic-book hero's. The lower part of his face looked as though it was made of steel. His eyes were an aquamarine, reminiscent of tropical seas, and they would have provided some softness to his face if he did not use them so piercingly.

"I can't leave Dunedin. I'm needed at work," I said. It came out as though I was a brain surgeon who needed to cope with a backlog of leucotomies.

"What exactly do you do?"

"I'm a travel consultant."

He folded his arms. He and his aquamarine eyes were not impressed. "What firm?"

"Bennet's," I said proudly, as though it was Thomas Cook's.

"I'm sure they'll be able to spare you for a few days," he said. "We just don't want you placing yourself in any more danger."

Placing myself in danger! I liked that.

"I haven't exactly enjoyed the last few days," I said.

"You refused a police escort from Invercargill," he said.

"I have assisted you to catch several dangerous criminals," I pointed out.

"And don't think we don't appreciate it. But you have also botched up a plan that has taken months to bring to fruition. We don't think you are in any further danger, but we want to be quite sure."

"I have a job I like very much — a job lots of people would like to have. I'm not prepared to jeopardise it. I'm sure my employer won't let me have any time off, even if I wanted to ask him. Which I don't."

He turned his laser beam gaze on Zoltan.

"I'll see you back at the station, Senior Sergeant. You're staying for lunch, I see."

"Yes, sir," Zoltan said, very smartly, hastily opening the door for him like a junior nurse for a hospital matron. I had caught that look between them. Zoltan was to persuade me to go into hiding.

"Don't say it." I said. "I'm not going anywhere."

"It would put my mind at rest if I could persuade you to go somewhere safe."

"It would also make a good impression on the Admiral of the Fleet," I said, gesturing after the Very Important Policeman.

"He's got nothing to do with it. I know now is not the time to say it, but I really care about what happens to you."

"You didn't really care at Stewart Island. You didn't care enough then to trust me."

He rolled his eyes towards the ceiling. "Why do I get this feeling that we are going to have this conversation every time you can't get your own way?"

"What?"

"I mean, when we have got all this business over, I intend to see a lot of you. After David's trial, when you can't think I have any ulterior motive." Zoltan said.

I needed time to digest this remark. I put The Cat's plate on the floor and watched while he ate it with gusto. After washing my hands I put some butter in the pan, chopped the parsley, mushrooms and bacon, added some sherry, then turned to face him.

"Supposing I could get a few days off. Where would I go? Apart from Rona, the only real friends I've got in Dunedin are the people in this house. If I stay at Rona's I might as well advertise it in the paper, she's got such a big mouth. If I go home to the farm and there's any danger, that means I could be placing my parents, and as it now happens, my grandparents in danger too."

"Well, we have places you can go," he said eagerly. "It would be better if you went to a safe house."

"Will you be there?" I asked.

"I could see. At the very least I could come and see you."

"Would they let you?" I asked.

"I shall insist," he said. "Especially if you want me to."

He came over to where I was poking the food about the pan with a plastic spatula. I felt his hands on my shoulders. Just as I was turning around, Peter entered the kitchen. "Mm, that smells good."

"Would you like to stay for lunch?" I asked, hoping he would say no, but he had the sensitivity of a vulture.

"Yes, please. I'm starving."

Zoltan made the tea, Peter made the toast, I set the table and dished out the food and we all tucked in.

"What time does your friend Christine get back tonight?" Peter asked, too casually.

"I'm not certain if she's coming back tonight."

"She said she was." he said.

"When?" I asked.

"Down at Stewart Island."

Lord, I thought, he must have made an impression. Christine was as secretive about her movements as the I.R.A..

I stared at him. I thought with envy how quickly they had hit it off, that half hour on the boat, jacking up a date. Everything straightforward and normal. I kept looking at him.

What did he see in Christine? What did Christine see in him?

Fascination is a funny thing, I thought.

"If Giselle goes to a safe house, what do you think of my chances of going with her?"

"Slender."

"Visiting?"

"Possible."

"I am going to insist," Zoltan declared.

Peter looked at him. Then he looked at me. I knew what he was thinking. He was wondering what Zoltan saw in me. It made me so happy, the way he tried not to look amazed. But he was Zoltan's friend and Zoltan had confided in him.

"Fascination's a funny thing, isn't it, Peter?" I asked. He went quite red, looked apologetic, then laughed.

"It makes the world go round." he said.

"That's love," I corrected him.

"Same thing," he said.

"Just as a matter of interest, what makes you think they won't let Zoltan guard me?" I asked.

"He's too valuable."

"Thank you. I'm flattered."

"What I mean is his job is to smash the drug ring. Someone else will be detailed to look after you."

When we had finished lunch we all puddled around doing the dishes. Peter went out of the room, saying, "I'll leave a note on the pad for Christine to ring me as soon as she gets back."

"Fair enough," I said.

Zoltan said unexpectedly, "Is it all right if I tell you I love you?"

"So long as it's true."

When he stepped over to me and put his arms around me, I said, "Do you realise you have only kissed me once?"

"To speak of love is to make love," he said.

"A policeman who quotes Balzac," I said.

Our lips had barely touched when Peter strode back in.

"I hope you and Christine manage to get a bit of privacy tonight," I said.

"I apologise, but Ma'am, we are on duty and it is definitely against regulations to kiss suspects, witnesses or innocent bystanders."

"Take him away," I said to Zoltan.

As I passed the telephone table I managed to sneak a look at the note he had left for Christine. It read, "You are wanted for questioning. Please telephone urgently. Love D.P.C. Peter Jenkins." He was going to be a droll rather than a romantic lover.

Zoltan decided to drive me to work, and as soon as I had packed my case, or rather re-packed it, we set off. I promised Zoltan that after I had typed my report on Stewart Island I would approach Mr Bennet about having a few days off. I was to telephone him when I was ready to leave for the safe house. He kissed me briefly before he drove off.

Rona was peering out the window when I got out of Zoltan's car.

"Gosh, who's that?" She asked as I swept in.

"Just one of my fans," I said. "Where's Mr Bennet?"

"Not back yet. I hope he isn't late, there's someone waiting for him in his office."

"Well, I'll finish my report," I said, sitting down at my desk and whipping the cover off my typewriter in order to forestall any questions.

Mr Bennet hurried through from the street. "Hullo, Giselle. How was your trip?"

"Not bad," I replied.

"Well, there's plenty of work there for you."

"There always is."

"There's someone waiting to see you in your office, Mr Bennet," Rona piped up immediately in the sycophantic tone she used to him.

He arranged his face into its most efficient expression and bustled in.

The report I made was shorter than might have been expected. Sometimes my reports are quite lyrical, but with the thought of asking for a few days off hanging over my head I was not quite up to deathless prose.

Just as I finished it the Very Important Policeman emerged from Mr Bennet's office, not at all perturbed by our stares.

"Miss Dougal," he said, acknowledging me with amused courtesy, half saluting and partly raising his resplendent cap as he went through the open door to the street.

"Giselle, can I see you a moment?" Mr Bennet called with unwonted benignity. I went into his office as one hypnotised. He sat me down.

He poured me some coffee from his own coffee machine in one of the posh cups that we were forbidden to use because they were for the exclusive use of important clients. I was too overcome to remind him that I didn't drink coffee.

"Now, Giselle, I've been thinking that you should have a few days off, paid of course — take as long as you like." He waved a pudgy hand expansively.

Only those who know Mr Bennet's parsimony, who have had to go through expense accounts with him while he clucks over every cent, and have had to remind him a pay-rise is due while he does everything but tear out his thinning hair, could understand my astonishment.

"You won't give my job to anyone?" I asked.

"Of course not," he said, managing to look aggrieved that I

should have suggested it. The Very Important Policeman must have been very persuasive.

"I understand you are helping the police," he asked, his eyes gleaming with curiosity. I was not very forthcoming. Obviously he had not been told any details.

"Not very much, I'm afraid. I've been more of a nuisance than anything else." I said. He hovered around me, longing to be confided in, not daring to ask.

"I'll tell you about it when it's all over, Mr Bennet. You'll be the first to know."

"Well, take care of yourself," he said, opening the door for me. I picked up my suitcase and said goodbye to the girls.

"I've got a few days off," I told them.

"Not again," Rona said.

"That's enough, Rona," Mr Bennet said, peremptorily. "Giselle isn't feeling well, are you, Giselle." And he nodded and winked and blinked in a manner so transparently conspiratorial that no-one believed him at all.

Instead of telephoning Zoltan immediately from the office I decided to get a few books from the Dunedin Public Library. If I was going to be cooped up for any length of time at least I could read to my heart's content.

It was while I was crossing the Octagon that I began to think I was being followed. While waiting at the traffic lights for the "cross now" signal, I turned my head with assumed nonchalance, but couldn't see anyone. Still, as I walked through the plaza to the library I felt a distinct sense of unease, a feeling of coldness from the nape of my neck to the base of my spine.

Just as I entered the library I looked behind me, the nonchalance not quite so easy to assume now. I couldn't see anyone. Or rather, I could see too many people, ducking into the shops in the plaza, taking shortcuts to the main street, and sunning themselves on the wooden benches.

Once in the library I hopped onto the escalator to head for the second floor for some biographies. Just before I stepped off the escalator I turned. The self-closing glass doors had just slid together behind a fat lady and I thought I saw a man in a dark suit gazing up at me from outside the entrance.

After choosing my books with less care than usual I went down by the stairs to the ground floor. The queue was long, and the library staff looked harrassed. I glanced around furtively. A woman looked at me oddly, disapprovingly, as though she suspected I might have library books secreted about my person that I did not intend to present for issue. At last I got to the top of the queue, tucked my stamped books under my arm and dithered in the entrance way. It occurred to me to telephone Zoltan from the Library.

I went to the public telephones, but they were all in use. I cursed all the people chatting about trivialities under the plastic soundproof bubbles.

When I emerged into the sunlight of the plaza I decided to get some more books from the Athenaeum Library. As I retraced my steps through the plaza I noticed a man in a dark suit reading a newspaper. I couldn't see his face. There were a lot of people reading and talking on the various seats.

As I crossed the Octagon I couldn't see anyone acting suspiciously, and when I got to the Athenaeum I chose some more books, novels this time, rather more calmly.

When I came out of the Athenaeum I saw, out of the corner of my eye, leaning against the lamp-post at the end of the Broadway Arcade, a big man in a dark suit with a folded newspaper in his hand.

Without faltering I headed into the women's rest-room. I could have telephoned Zoltan from there but it occurred to me that if in fact the man in the dark suit was following me, he would follow both of us if Zoltan came to pick me up. Or at the very least he would know that the police were protecting me. I was not entirely certain that it was a good thing for him to know this.

I knew that on fine days the fire escape door in the women's rest-room was left open. I headed towards it and down the iron steps, aware that one of the attendants was watching me with an expression of baffled rage. At the bottom of the steps was a vast concrete yard full of large cardboard boxes.

Trucks of various sizes were parked here and there. There was a steep narrow drive-way which I hurried up, hugging the side as goods vans squeezed past me, all the drivers whistling at me the way they feel obliged to whistle at every woman between sixteen and sixty.

I nipped across Moray Place then down Burlington Street, grateful that it was as steep as a ski-slope. There was, mercifully, a public phone box just where it connected with the Queen's Gardens. I dialled 111, as I had no two cent pieces. The operator found Zoltan for me at once.

"Zoltan, I think I was followed."

"Where are you?" He asked. I told him. In one minute he was with me. As soon as he opened the car door I leapt in. I told him what had happened. He didn't say anything about my not telephoning him from work as I was supposed to.

"What did this man look like?"

"I don't know — he was never very close. He was big and he had on a dark suit. I'm not even completely sure he *was* following me."

"He probably was," Zoltan said. "Perhaps it's just as well you went up to the library. They've shown their hand now."

"Where are you taking me?"

"Not far. Out to Doctor's Point." he said.

"Oh, I like it out there, don't you?"

"In happier circumstances."

"Why do they want me? I haven't done anything." I said.

"Revenge possibly. You messed up a big deal for them, remember. Or maybe they just don't like leaving any loose ends. They could have other reasons for wanting you."

"Such as?"

"I don't know, it's just an idea, but they may have wanted to take you and then trade you for David."

"Would the police do that?" I asked.

"I'm not sure," he said, although I'm sure he did know. I wondered whether they would consider it a fair trade.

"Won't it be nice out at Doctor's Point, alone together?" I said.

"We won't exactly be alone," he said. "And I'm afraid I won't be able to stay long."

9

Not Alone

We certainly were not alone. We arrived at the safe house, which was hidden in tall bush off a steep road. Just inside the gate, two policemen skulked in a hide like duck-shooters.

When we entered the house which was white and two-storeyed, we found two policemen and a policewoman. They were all armed, even Koa, a pretty young Maori woman there to act as chaperone as much as anything else. Koa took me upstairs to an enormous bedroom with three beds.

"You and I sleep here," she said. "One of the men will be outside the door all night."

I unpacked my clothes and we went back downstairs to join the others. The sight of them with their shoulder holsters and their two-way radios gave me great confidence, although I doubted very much if anyone would find us.

Within a few minutes Peter arrived with Mrs Livingston. We greeted each other very affectionately.

"Isn't this exciting!" she exclaimed, to the amusement of all the police. Mrs Livingston was to share the large bedroom with Koa and me.

There was a house telephone and I called my parents to inform them that I had arrived safely and that I was back at work.

One of the policemen, whose name was Darryl, had a game of scrabble with Mrs Livingston and Koa, while Zoltan and I played chess in a desultory fashion, holding hands and gazing at each other. We were not encouraged to go outside, in spite of the fact that the house, or certainly the ground floor, was not visible from any of the roads.

Zoltan and Peter were not part of our guard. Around two-thirty they went back to the police station. Any feeling of excitement disappeared when they left, and the thought of not being allowed to go out for a breath of fresh air brought on a feeling of claustrophobia.

Koa read a book until it was time for afternoon tea, which she and I made for everyone. Even doing the dishes was a welcome break.

Darryl and the other policeman, whose name was Bob, spent a lot of time peering furtively out the windows and talking on their hand telephones to the men at the gate.

Koa, Mrs Livingston and I decided to prepare roast lamb for dinner. The house was well-stocked with food. There were shelves crammed with tinned and packaged food, plus a fridge and freezer bulging with meat, ice-cream and vegetables.

"Are we here for a long siege?" I asked Koa. I supposed the first-name basis we were on from the beginning was because of this.

"Not necessarily," she replied. "This place always has to be ready at a moment's notice. The locals think it's an ordinary weekend bach. If a crowd of people arrived out here carrying masses of food people might talk, and when people talk one never knows who's listening. That's why we all arrived out here at different times."

Bob and Darryl changed places with the men at the gate immediately after dinner, which we ate early out of sheer boredom. Zoltan arrived back about seven, having finished his shift for the day. To my surprise Peter, who was also off-duty, turned up with Christine in tow. To my great delight she had brought Charlie with her.

"He was waiting on the doorstep for you. He won't be missed for a couple of hours. I'll take him back with me when I go."

One of the men who had been at the gate went to sleep on a cot-bed in the lounge, as they were going to work in shifts. The other produced a guitar from his bedroom and began to sing country and western songs in a mournful voice that sounded exactly like an old gramophone record.

Although it was still quite light, Zoltan and I sneaked away and went for a walk through the several acres that were fenced off around the house. Charlie padded along behind us, knocking his big head against our legs. We held hands as we turned up a narrow, barely used path, surprising a litter of kittens about four weeks old. The mother cat, a domestic cat turned wild, appeared from nowhere and placed herself in front of them with her back arched, a skinny bundle of courage. As we turned away from them, a kitten who had been a few yards away from us hurried past us with comical stealth.

"Has David said anything, you know, to help you?"

"We couldn't get much out of him today, but we will. He had his lawyer with him when I left."

"He isn't the main one. He was amused, and sort of flattered when I said we called him Mr X," I said.

"We know that. What we don't know is where the head of the

organisation, the real Mr X, is." Zoltan frowned. "The chances are that he's scarpered by now. We don't know if he's in New Zealand, Australia or somewhere else entirely."

We came to a small creek and stopped. I leaned against a tree trunk and Zoltan stood a couple of feet from me, holding an overhanging branch with one hand.

Although I had realised that Zoltan was not quite as wise, as noble and Godlike as I had at first thought, I was not any less in love with him for all that. His lack of conceit, his kindness to Mrs Roberts and Mrs Livingston, his steadfastness of purpose were genuine attributes that I knew would last if I ever grew accustomed to his handsome looks, difficult as it was to imagine that happening.

There was such a stillness in the bush, we talked in whispers. I turned to him like a flower turning to the sun and then I was in his arms feeling his magical kiss on my lips, and my eyes and my throat.

"I bought something for you when I was in town," Zoltan said. In his hand was a tiny box which he opened, displaying a diamond ring with a coloured stone in the centre.

"Will you wear it?" He asked.

"Will I!" I said, holding out my left hand without any false modesty.

Zoltan laughed happily, exultantly. Charlie turned his sweet, ugly face toward him, wagging his tail thumpily on the ground. Although we could have stayed out there for hours clinging to each other, Zoltan was a great one for obeying rules and regulations, and he suggested that we go back in. We found Christine and Peter snogging passionately on a wicker couch on the verandah.

"Come in and have a drink with us, we've just got engaged,"

Zoltan said, and they disentangled themselves and followed us into the house. The ring was admired by everyone. The coloured stone I could now see was a garnet, my lucky stone.

Christine said to us, "But you've only known each other a few days," with such a bright-eyed, meaningful look at Peter that everyone laughed.

Peter produced a bottle of whiskey and we all had a celebratory drink. Christine and I offered to make supper before Zoltan left. Mrs Livingston said, "I won't stay up for supper, I'm very tired. I think I'll go up to bed. I hope I can sleep after all this excitement. I forgot to bring my sleeping tablets."

Koa went to the medicine cabinet in the bathroom, returning with a bottle of dark brown liquid. She poured some into a medicine glass, saying, "There aren't any tablets but here's a sedative for you, Mrs Livingston."

"It looks like the stuff that turned Dr Jekyll into Mr Hyde," Zoltan said.

"It tastes like it, too," Mrs Livingston replied after she had tossed it down.

Koa took her upstairs, returning to ask if Christine and I needed any help in the kitchen. While the kettle was boiling I took some meat out of the fridge. When I had cut it and fed Charlie I said, "Christine, there are some pretty hungry cats out there. I'll take some of this meat out to them. I won't be a minute."

"O.K.," she said. She was much more malleable since meeting Peter. A week ago she would have accused me of trying to get out of helping with the supper.

I opened the kitchen door and Charlie trotted out ahead of me. With difficulty we found the path leading to the mother cat. Dusk was gathering and I wished I'd brought a torch. So that we wouldn't frighten the mother cat, we crept along for several minutes. Then we waited, hoping to see the kitten. Charlie had always been interested in cats and other animals, and I had not seen him act violently towards another creature.

There was an enormous packingcase with its back towards me and I assumed the cats had made their home in there. It was some time before they appeared, following the mother cat. They stopped when they saw us. I threw the meat gently towards them. Torn between hunger and fear, the mother cat waited. Charlie watched with interest from beside me. Realizing that she wouldn't take the meat while we were there I turned round and headed back.

The house was almost in darkness, as all the curtains were half-drawn. I had almost got there when I saw four men approaching the house. Thinking it was another changing of the guard, I was about to call out to them when I noticed a certain sneakiness in their demeanour. They went into the kitchen and I saw Christine look up in surprise at the first man and in great fear at the other three. They waved her through at gun-point to the lounge where the others were.

Utterly uncertain what to do I crept forward to the verandah, Charlie at my heels. If I crouched down and twisted myself around I could peek through the tiny piece of window not covered by the curtain, which had been left open slightly to let the fresh air in.

I could only see two of the men since the curtain obscured some of the room, but I recognised one of them as the man in the brown suit who had followed me from the library.

It was just not possible that he had followed Zoltan and me. He had been nowhere about when we met at the Queens Gardens, and even if he had been, Zoltan had driven all round the houses before finally heading to Doctor's Point.

Now that I could see him close up, I recognised him. I had seen the man in the dark brown suit around the town from time to time, in the coffee-bars, at the pictures, different places. He was an ordinary looking person, a bit tough-looking, not entirely respectable, but able to walk in the light of common day without arousing comment of any kind. But the second man was like some monster hidden away somewhere and allowed out on just such occasions as this. I will never be able to erase the memory of that man from my mind. His face was large but bony and above his narrow hooked nose, slanting eyes exactly the colour of a crocodile's glared out at the world. Those apparently lashless eyes had precisely the same intent and merciless look I had intercepted in the eyes of a cat watching a bird.

He was tall and hefty, but pound for pound, inch for inch he was not taller or heftier than Peter or the other two policemen in the room. But his air of barely bridled menace added a supernatural dimension to his presence. The blood had frozen in my veins at the sight of him and all present in the room had blanched, even Peter whose bumptious courage should have been proof against anything. I wondered if the frightening man was Mr X, but he, along with everyone else in the room, was looking at someone I could not see.

"You're not as clever as you thought you were," That someone was saying in a quiet, posh voice that set my heart thumping. I recognised the voice. I strained to see who was on the other side of the room but was still unable.

"How did you find us?" Peter asked, probably not expecting a reply.

"Which one of you is Peter Jenkins?" The familiar voice

asked, and when Peter indicated who he was by a movement of his head, it went on, "Thank you for leaving the note on the telephone pad. When you picked up Christine we followed you. Where's the farmer's daughter?" The voice finished abruptly.

When no one answered, the owner of the voice took a step forward, straight into my line of vision. I had to stifle a gasp. No wonder the voice had sounded familiar! It was none other than Leo Thompson, our landlord. Leo's son, Andrew, a sulky inarticulate lout, stood behind him.

"Giselle's upstairs is she?" He was saying. Again no one answered. "How about the old lady, where is she?"

"She's upstairs asleep," Koa said in a frightened voice.

"Get her down here," he said. The man in the brown suit followed Koa upstairs and very quickly they returned with a drowsy but startled Mrs Livingston.

"Good Heavens, who is that?" She cried. Leo laughed. It was the first time I had heard him laugh. It was a low and malicious sound.

"They're all frightened of you, Harry," he said to the monster. It seemed incredible that he had a name (did Frankenstein's monster have a name?) and such an ordinary, good-sounding name like Harry. Harry was neither offended, surprised nor amused by Mrs Livingston's reaction. Perhaps he was used to it.

Obviously the thing for me to do was to creep down to Bob and Darryl at the gate. As I stepped back my hand must have touched the Dutch blind. It shot up, exposing me to their startled gaze.

"Get her!" Leo shouted. "No, not you."

Rushing down the path I wondered who was chasing me — the man in the brown suit, Andrew or Harry?

Whoever was following me was bigger than me but he didn't jog every day, and besides, I was younger. I got to the hide at the gate in record time. Bob was slouched in a corner, bashed on the head, and Darryl was stretched out on the grass unconscious or dead. My mind was frozen in a momentary icy panic as I ducked behind the hide.

My pursuer stopped a few feet away from me, knowing that I could only be behind the hide, even if he couldn't tell where I was by the loud thumping of my heart. When he took a step closer I saw by the light of the moon that it was the man in the brown suit.

He pointed his gun at where I was standing, saying, "You might as well come out. You'll save us both a lot of trouble."

Partly out of relief that it was he and not the one called Harry, I came out, followed by Charlie. If I had been braver I might have made a dash for it in the darkness, but I didn't think I would get very far.

Charlie, who was used to charging about hiding with me and from me during our games in the park, wagged his tail at the man, who surprisingly bent and patted him.

We returned to the house and Leo smiled rather smugly, "Good evening, Miss Dougal — how's your cat?" It was typical of his pettiness to allude to The Cat at this moment, letting me know that he had always been aware that we had adopted The Cat.

We were told to sit down. Harry, Andrew and the man in the brown suit who we soon discovered was called Colin, placed themselves at each of the doors, gun in hand, while Leo stood confidently unarmed in front of us. They had disarmed Peter and the others, piling their guns on the china cabinet on which Leo now leaned, chunkily suave.

"What I intend to do is exchange you lot for David." he said.

"They won't do that," Peter said, when nobody else spoke.

"I think they might," Leo said. "After all, there's nothing in the papers yet about it; they're keeping it all quiet. We've got plenty of time. You gentlemen come in here with me so we can talk privately. Let's see if we can come to some accommodation on this matter. Watch the ladies, Colin." Indicating that the three policemen should go with him, he went into the kitchen. Koa and Mrs Livingston and Christine were left sitting on the sofa like three monkeys on a stick, while I knelt in front of them with my arms around Charlie. Colin self-consciously kept his pistol trained on us, like an actor with stage-fright.

After a few moments of utter silence, punctuated only by Charlie's registration and name medals jangling against each other every time he moved his head, I got an idea. I had never met Charlie's owners. I was not entirely certain that they knew that he went jogging with Frey and me each morning, although I assumed they did. Certainly they wouldn't know me by name. How would they react if I telephoned and said I had their dog and was keeping him out all night? I patted Charlie while I surreptitiously memorised the telephone number on his name medal.

"Would you mind if I telephoned the owners of the dog just to let them know that he won't be home tonight? They'll be a bit worried if I don't take him back."

Colin was not used to acting on his own initiative. For some time now he had had the air of a man who had let himself in for more than he had bargained for. He cast an uncertain look at the door leading to the kitchen where Leo Thompson was.

"How do I know you won't try any tricks?"

"Well, you dial the number and I'll speak to them," I said.

"How will I know it's only them you're speaking to?" He asked, suspiciously. I pretended to think for a moment, but not too long in case he enquired what their name was.

"Their telephone number is probably on his collar," I said, pretending to notice for the first time. "Yes, here it is, Dunedin 36-385."

Colin peered at the name tag.

"I don't know what you're bothering about the dog for," Christine said suddenly, in her superior, interfering way. Now that Colin had almost made a decision he was not going to have anyone complicating the process.

"I'm in charge here," he told her. "She's quite right. It's no good having the people worrying about their dog. She can ring if she likes."

I moved to the phone and Colin watched as I dialled. A woman's voice answered, faintly irritated, as though the phone had rung in the middle of her favourite television programme.

"It's Giselle Dougal speaking," I said very clearly, injecting a great deal of warmth into my voice so that Colin wouldn't suspect the person at the other end hadn't the faintest idea who I was.

"Who is it?" the woman asked, but I knew she had heard my name.

"I just rang to say that Christine and I won't be able to get Charlie back tonight."

"What the hell are you talking about?" It was gratifying to hear the righteous anger gathering in her voice. "If you've got our dog, bring him back immediately or I'll ring the police."

"We're staying overnight at a friend's place," I said.

"I mean what I say — I'll ring the police!" the woman shouted furiously.

"I'd be so grateful if you would. I'll bring him back sometime tomorrow, goodbye," I said sweetly.

"Thank you very much. That's put their minds at rest," I said to Colin, as I sat on the floor again.

Would the enraged lady ring the police? Would the policeman who answered her be amused enough, or annoyed enough to mention it to his colleagues so that it trickled back, quickly, to Zoltan or the higher-ups at the station? And would they put two and two together? Would they know it was a cry for help? Would Charlie's owners charge down to the station, filled with ire and demand to see the superintendent? Would Zoltan have proudly announced that he had just got engaged and would he have mentioned my name? Or would Charlie's owners merely return to watching television and content themselves with the thought of how they would tick me off when I returned with him tomorrow.

After about half an hour the others came back into the room.

"What about making us all a cup of tea?" Leo Thompson said, chiefly to me, because I had never made him welcome at our house. Christine and I got up to go to the kitchen.

"They've got some nerve," she said, when we were out of earshot in the kitchen. "We're not servants."

"One of the principal duties of a captive is to get the food and drink ready, in my experience." I said. We went back in with tea and biscuits, which we put on the coffee table in the lounge.

"Just sit down again where we can keep an eye on you," Leo Thompson said, adding in his insufferable way, "I'll be mother."

We all sat around sipping tea and politely passing biscuits, while he stood in front of us like a lecturer, and explained what he intended doing, for all the world as though it was a small town meeting of the Travel Club or Overseas League.

He was dressed in his usual natty but unsuitable gear, the gold pendant round his neck gleaming occasionally above his pure silk lilac shirt, the pokerwork leather belt cinched too tightly around his thick waist, his well-cut trousers encasing his stubby legs.

"What I intend on doing is this. I'm going to offer all of you alive in exchange for David. One of you will be allowed to take our terms to the police." I thought his gaze rested on Christine for a moment, remembering the coffee and lemonade she had always offered him on his visits. He went on, "You can decide between you who it is. We are going to shoot the lot of you if there is any trouble, or any haggling. They'd better understand that."

Peter said, "The guy we would have to speak to is away on another case. I happen to know that. He simply won't be available until morning, or at least until very late this evening."

"Well, I'm prepared to wait until morning. David's seen his lawyers so they won't get any information out of him in a hurry."

"How can you all get away?" Christine asked. "What about your wife?"

"Don't worry, we've got all that sorted out," Leo Thompson said.

"Haven't you heard, Christine?" I said. "The family that slays together stays together."

"And you," Leo Thompson said, "can shut up. You'll be the first to get it, I can tell you that."

There was a long silence after that while Leo Thompson got himself together again. For a man who liked to give the impression of airy confidence he was very easily put off his stroke.

At last he said, "Well you might as well go to bed anyway, you women. Andrew, you take them up. If they get cute, kill them."

Andrew brightened considerably at the prospect. Sometimes he had been sent to mow our lawn when David and Tim had been away, a task he had performed in a dispirited fashion. On those occasions it would have been a compliment to describe him as dull-normal.

Us women, accompanied by Charlie, all got up to go, followed by the wordless Andrew who stood at the bedroom door. We didn't get undressed because he hadn't closed the door, and was peering at us with an expression of sly lechery.

Mrs Livingston was the only one who wanted to sleep. She hopped into bed and lay there staring at us, as pathetic as an abandoned puppy.

"I don't think I'll be able to sleep," she said. "I wish I could have some more of that sedative."

"I'll get you some," Koa said, moving swiftly to the door.

"I'm just going down to get a sedative for Mrs Livingston," she said to Andrew, expecting him to stand aside.

Andrew shifted the gun from one hand to the other, then quite casually took Koa by the throat and began to choke her. Christine was the nearest and she stepped towards them and tried to pull Koa away. There was a large brass vase on the bedside table. I picked it up and swung it at Andrew's head.

Koa had gone an awful colour. Andrew let her go and turned to me. I stepped back. Charlie leapt at Andrew's throat. Goofy, gentle Charlie of the perennially wagging tail was suddenly transformed, the hackles risen stiffly from his neck to his tail. I had had no idea his teeth, now bared in a snarl, were so enormous.

The gun dropped from Andrew's hand. Koa grabbed it and

shot him in the back of the head. The silencer made it a plopping sound. He fell across Mrs Livingston's bed. Too shocked to scream, she scrambled out of the bed. We all stood, huddled in the middle of the room, expecting a rush of men up the stairs, but they hadn't heard a thing.

"When I telephoned about Charlie before, I did it because I thought his owners might telephone the police. Do you think if they do that the police will understand?" I asked Koa.

She looked very doubtful. "I shouldn't think so," she said. "Only if Zoltan hears about it, and there's no reason why he should. The police won't be worried about a dog who's going to be returned tomorrow anyway."

"But I'm not supposed to have their dog," I said.

"We would be too busy to deal with something like that," she said, haughtily. "Especially as you did say the dog would be returned tomorrow anyway."

I sat down on the bed, saw Andrew's body and stood up again.

"One of us has to get out of here and get to a phone. If we all go they'll hear us. Mrs Livingston can't come anyway." I said.

"Well, I'll stay here. I'm supposed to be guarding you all. I'll look after Mrs Livingston," Koa said. I would have liked Christine to come with me, but it would be better if only Charlie and I went in case we met one of Leo Thompson's men on the stairs.

"If I meet one of them I'll say Charlie wants to pee."

"Well, take the gun," Koa said.

"No, you keep it. Lock yourselves in. If I run into them it's better if I don't have it. If I don't run into them I won't need it."

After wiping the blood off Charlie I crept down the stairs, Charlie pattering behind me. The noise of the television and the conversation of the men covered any small sounds we might have made. Although he was in the habit of barking joyously when setting off for a run, Charlie had the good sense to refrain from doing so on this occasion, so we got out the kitchen door safely. At the bottom of the path we passed the recumbent bodies of the two policemen. If they weren't dead it would eventually occur to Leo Thompson to tie them up or take them into the house, so I hurried on.

Pursued by terror, Charlie and I reached the road. It was very dark. There were no street lights. In the space of ten minutes three cars passed us. The first flashed by so quickly the occupants didn't see us, and a lone woman in the second car gave me a frightened look then accelerated hastily. The third car was driven by an elderly man, keeping well within the speed limit. When I called out he stopped and I ran up to the open front window.

"Could you please give me a lift to the nearest telephone box?" I asked. He was a small, conservatively dressed, innocent-looking man. He could have been a lay preacher.

"What are you doing out here at this time of night?" he enquired sententiously.

"I have to get the police. Please help me."

After regarding me doubtfully and the blood-speckled Charlie even more so he said, "Get in, then."

We got in and it seemed to take him forever to start the car again. He was a real Sunday driver. I began to think I could have got to a phone faster on foot. All his concentration seemed necessary just for driving the car so I didn't tell him very much.

"Could you go a bit faster, please? I'm in a terrific hurry!" I said.

"It's better to be five minutes late in this world than twenty years early in the next," he informed me. By the look of him he would have a fund of remarks like that.

"It really is a matter of life and death. There are some drug dealers in a house back there, and two policemen either dead or badly wounded. I was lucky to escape."

From his look of puzzled disbelief I might as well have told him I was running from aliens in a spaceship.

The occasional houses we passed had no lights, and even if they had been occupied probably had no telephones. Not many people had telephones in their weekend baches. It seemed wiser to stay with the slow old man than rush up to a house that was probably empty.

Finally we saw a telephone box spotlighted by a solitary streetlamp at the side of the road. As soon as I pointed it out to the old man he stopped about twenty feet from it. I thanked him and leapt out, to his great relief. It may have been my imagination but the car seemed to start quite quickly this time and he headed off over the hill at a great bat.

Unfortunately the light was the only thing about the telephone box that was working. The phone itself had been vandalised. I resisted an urge to fling myself on the ground and weep. The darkness was eerily silent and I was glad of Charlie's company. Ghostly hands seemed to stretch out from the darkness and shadows merged and parted.

Just as we were about to head off into the blackness a small convoy of cars appeared in the distance, travelling at great speed. Charlie and I stood waiting in the little patch of light. When they all stopped and Zoltan stepped out of the first car to my own surprise I burst into tears of relief. "Did you get my message?"

"Well, a very angry taxpayer came down to the station complaining about two young women taking her dog. Said one of them was Giselle Dougal. What's happened?"

"Quite a lot. We were all being held hostage. You'll never guess who your famous Mr X is! Our landlord, Leo Thompson. He arrived with three others. Just crept up. They've killed the two policemen at the gate. At least I think they have."

Zoltan told one of the others to radio for ambulances.

"Who is in the house now?" He asked.

"Well, we had to shoot Andrew Thompson. He tried to choke Koa when he was sent to guard us in the bedroom. There's Leo Thompson, and you remember the man who followed me? He's there and his name is Colin, I think he's relatively harmless. And there's the most awful man called Harry. He never says a word, just stands there looking predatory."

"So Christine, and Koa and Mrs Livingston are upstairs in the end bedroom?" Zoltan asked.

"Yes, and all the men are downstairs talking. Peter told Leo Thompson that the head of the Drug Squad wouldn't be available until the morning. Just playing for time, I suppose. I mean I presume he can be reached somehow."

"Are they all armed?"

"Except for Leo Thompson. I think he considers himself too superior of a person to carry a gun. It would spoil his image and I'm sure he wouldn't know how to use one. But the remaining two are armed." I said.

"Well, we'll have to get into the house quietly and take them by surprise." Zoltan said.

We got into his car and the whole convoy set off for the house, but about a hundred yards before we got there I was left in the care of two policemen who were decidedly peeved at being left out of the action.

There were brief whispered discussion into the hand-phones

and then about twenty police officers disappeared silently through the gate.

However there was no shoot-out at the O.K. Corral that night. An ambulance arrived and took the two men from the gate away. Shortly after that there was a general exodus. Christine came running up to the car I was in.

"What a time we've had," she gasped. "Leo Thompson came upstairs with cigarettes for Andrew. When he found he was dead he started shouting. Koa had left the gun on the other side of the room so he grabbed it. When the others saw that Andrew was dead, they tied us all up and then they all rushed off."

"They must have been in one of the cars that passed while I was in the old man's car on the way to the phone box," I said.

So there it was. We were free, but so were they. Zoltan, although relieved that Christine, Koa and Mrs Livingston were safe, was visibly disappointed that he had not yet caught Mr X.

The senior police officer insisted that Mrs Livingston had to go to the Dunedin Public Hospital to be kept under observation for the night. Christine and Peter followed our car to the station and we all had to help with identikit pictures of Leo Thompson, Harry and Colin. Peter was quite experienced at describing people, at least for police purposes. Christine and I were both quite expert at mimicking people and were crestfallen that no-one was interested in our ability to impersonate him, except Zoltan who was the only one of our little coterie who hadn't actually seen him.

While we were all sitting and discussing Leo Thompson, we heard a muffled explosion and the sound of shattered glass and splintered wood.

Someone came rushing in to tell us that a home-made bomb

had been thrown in the window of David's cell. Only the fact that the door of his cell had been left open because of the extreme heat of the evening had saved him. As soon as the bomb hurtled through the bars of his cell, David, with great presence of mind, had picked it up, thrown it into the corridor and slammed his cell door seconds before it exploded, scattering huge sharp nails and gunpowder.

Zoltan and Peter hurried to the cells and we went with them. It was the first time in living memory that the smile had been wiped from David's face. White and shaken, he was moved to another, safer cell. A doctor was sent for, he was pronounced unhurt, accepted a sedative, and after maintaining a terse silence for a few minutes he remarked, "It seems that I am no longer universally loved."

Zoltan said, "That was your friend, Leo Thompson."

"That's what you are surmising, is it?"

"You don't think I'm right?" Zoltan asked.

"Well, Leo will be behind it, of course, but he never does his own dirty work, you know." David said.

"I don't know. Tell me."

The smile, toothy, but diffident was beginning to reappear. "If I do, does that mean I get immunity from prosecution?" he asked.

"Your best course is to tell us all you know. The judge is the one who decides how much it will go in your favour. I'd say the more you talk the better off you will be. There won't be much point in their killing you after you've spilled the beans, you know."

"But," David persisted, "can I turn state's evidence? Do I have your word that I'll be taken care of?"

"Just talk," Zoltan said. "We'll see what it's worth when we've heard what you have to say."

Two inspectors arrived then, and they decided they would take David's statement. They instructed Zoltan to find Leo Thompson. They also instructed him to get Christine and me out of the way. Just as we were leaving, Colin was brought in, covered in blood and grazes.

"Who's this?" Zoltan asked.

"It's Colin," I supplied.

"Hullo, Miss," Colin said, apparently glad to see a friendly face. "That Harry, he shoved me right out of the car! Right in front of a police vehicle."

"That's right," one of the policemen said.

"After they threw that home-made bomb into Tallintyre's cell we pursued them. The other one pushed him out the door and drove off. We had to pull up. There's another squad car after him, of course."

"Well, take him along to Inspector Kirby," Zoltan told him.

Zoltan and Peter decided to take Christine and me home. There were police cars scooting off in all directions. Just as we were leaving the station, my brother Alistair appeared on the steps.

"Giselle," he said, his voice quavering with relief.

"It's like Piccadilly Circus. If I stay here long enough I'll meet everyone I've ever known," I said.

After I had introduced them, Alistair said to Zoltan, "I was a bit worried about Giselle. She told me about all these drug pushers she's got mixed up with. I thought I'd come down to the station and see what was going on."

Zoltan gave me a tight-lipped look, so Alistair said quickly, "It's all right, I haven't told anyone else. I thought she should have someone from her family with her."

"Well, I'm practically family now." Zoltan said.

Alistair gaped. "Quick work, wasn't it?"

"The circumstances were extenuating." Zoltan answered.

"Well, congratulations, anyway," Alistair said.

"We are just about to run the girls home," Zoltan told him. "We've caught two of the gang, but another two are still out there somewhere."

"I could help you," Alistair said eagerly. "I've brought my gun."

"Thanks for the offer, but we can't let civilians in on a police operation. Still, you'll be staying with the girls, won't you? That'll be a help. We won't have to leave one of our men to look after them now."

"You think they are still after the girls?"

"No, it's highly unlikely. Their chief concern will be trying to get out of the country. We're watching all the ports and airports. We've set up road-blocks on all the main roads."

While they were talking we had moved to the cars. Zoltan and I went in the police car and Christine followed with Alistair and Peter.

When we arrived Zoltan telephoned to find out if they had got any information out of Colin, but he knew nothing. As I had thought, he was just called in at the last minute to lend a bit of muscle for a couple of hundred dollars.

Poor Peter was given the unenviable task of taking Charlie home. He returned all red in the face.

While Zoltan had been talking, the rest of us had huddled around the telephone. He was disappointed at the way things were going. It looked as though Leo Thompson might get away. The door of Tim's room opened and he stood leaning against it.

"Looking for Leo Thompson? I think I can help you." he said. Tim was hardly recognisable. It was the first time we had seen him in a suit, and he had shaved and had his hair cut.

"How come you know so much?" Zoltan asked, suspiciously.

"I'm Tim Sutton of the New South Wales Police Narcotics Branch."

"You can prove that, I suppose?"

Tim produced an I.D. which seemed to satisfy Zoltan. He was not, however, mollified. "I knew of course that the Australian police were working on this case. You've been lying pretty low, haven't you? A bit of co-operation earlier could have been helpful."

"Our information was that a member of your department was one of the drug ring," Tim said promptly. "That's why I decided to play it close to the chest."

"That was me," Zoltan said. "I've been working undercover. It's reassuring to know my cover held."

Tim opened his mouth to say something, but Zoltan cut him off, saying, "You said you know where Leo Thompson is?"

"Yeah. I've got his car and his home phone and the phone here bugged, but they have been very careful. They must just use public phone boxes. It wasn't until just now I found out who Mr X is."

"We've known Leo Thompson is Mr X for a couple of days," Christine said, as though she herself had uncovered this information.

"Oh, it isn't Leo Thompson. There's someone else. I knew Leo was taking orders from another person. That's why I got Christine to give me a lift when we met and why I told her I was looking for a room. But they were so careful. I knew when the heat was on he'd panic and get in touch with his boss."

"Who is it?" Zoltan asked.

"Well, let's just say that you're not the undercover police officer we were tipped off about. It appears our Mr X is Assistant Commissioner Michael Lockwood."

"You're quite sure?" Zoltan asked, frowning. "That's a very serious accusation."

"You can hear the tapes for yourself if you like, Leo's up at Lockwood's Dunedin residence with him now. They're going to lie low for a bit." He opened his door to show all that electronic gear he prized so much. "It's all on the tapes."

"We'll hear them later. Let's get on and arrest them," Zoltan said.

"Did you know David was in the drug ring, too, Tim?" I asked.

"Not until I came here," Tim answered.

Zoltan rang the station, and we heard him directing all the cars to Michael Lockwood's house where Leo mistakenly thought he was safe. Zoltan, Tim and Peter left together looking very pleased with themselves.

"See you later, girls. See you again, Alistair," Zoltan said, remembering to be polite to his future brother-in-law.

As soon as they had gone, we all made for the kitchen.

"When you think about it, the police are just as devious as the crooks," Christine said. "I mean look at the way Tim sneaked his way in here, pretending to be a hitch-hiker, knowing that Leo Thompson owned this house. And Leo making out to Tim that he had met David accidentally at the pub when he knew him all along."

"I know. Nothing will surprise me now. Even if I go to work tomorrow and find out that Mr Bennet is a colonel in the KGB I won't bat an eyelid."

"You know you'll have to tell Mum and Dad about this before

it gets into the papers," Alistair said, sipping hot chocolate and eating cheese on toast.

"Yes, *I'll* tell Mum and Dad about this before it gets into the papers," I warned him. His great failing was that he liked to be the first with any news.

"How soon will you be getting married?" Christine was dying to know.

"I suppose we'll have to wait until all this blows over. Neither of us will want to spend our honeymoon sitting in a courtroom." I said. I made a mental note to meet Errol for lunch next week to brag about Zoltan and me and show off my ring. I wondered if Errol would ask to bring Tandy to the wedding.

"How many bridesmaids will you have?" Christine asked, cocking her head sideways, the way she does when she is being shrewd. This was a hint for me to ask her to be a bridesmaid, as she was assuming that Peter would be a groomsman at the wedding. Even if he wanted to, Peter would not have much chance of getting away from her.

"Well, I'll have Rona," I said slowly, adding, when her face fell, "and you, of course." This led to a lengthy discussion on bridesmaid's dresses which sent Alistair yawning to bed.

Christine and I stayed talking for another ten minutes, then crept past David's room where we could see through the open door that Alistair was sound asleep. We had decided to sleep in my room where there was a spare bed because (although neither of us were prepared to admit it) we were both feeling a bit nervous. We got undressed and into bed still planning weddings.

After a while I got up to go to the toilet. As I passed his room I noticed that Alistair's door was now shut. A noise, like wood moving against wood, caught my attention. I crept back to my bedroom.

"I think something's wrong. Alistair's door is shut and I can hear a noise."

"That doesn't mean anything," Christine said, with more hope than conviction, slithering out of bed. "Let's go and get the neighbours."

"No. We haven't time. Let's get the gun."

Alistair had put his rifle in the broom cupboard. We crept along the hall. The click of the catch on the broom cupboard door seemed very loud and sharp, so we didn't dare close it again. We had a whispered consultation, then Christine opened the door of Alistair's room, and I stood back pointing the rifle. Christine tip-toed over to the bed. Alistair was lying on his back.

"It's O.K. He's asleep," she said. "Put the light on."

With the light on we could see that Alistair's eyes were open, and we wondered why he didn't speak. Christine pulled the blankets back. Alistair was bound hand and foot and gagged with a grubby handkerchief. He began rolling his eyes upwards and sideways. There was a chair in the middle of the room and when we looked up we saw Harry staring down at us from the small trap door in the ceiling. I had known it was there because David and Leo Thompson had been up there once discussing the possibility of putting bats in the ceiling for insulation. At least that's what they'd said. I realised now that David had probably stashed some heroin up there. Or Harry thought he had.

It will be a long time before I forgive Christine for what she did next. She hopped right out through the open window and ran off into the darkness. I aimed the rifle at Harry and pressed the trigger. That's when I found that it wasn't loaded. By this time Harry had turned himself round and was lowering himself down from the opening in the ceiling.

As one of his feet touched the chair I knocked it away. He either lost his grip on the ceiling or deliberately let go, and he fell on the floor in a heap. I hit him on his bony head with the butt of the rifle. As I turned to run for my life, out of the corner of my eye, I saw him stand up, quivering like an enraged bull.

When I ducked behind the open door of the broom cupboard he charged out of the bedroom and through the gap between the hinges I could see him teetering on the little step that separated the cupboard from the hall, peering into the darkness where he thought I was hiding. I stepped around the door, kicked him in the backside so that he stumbled forward, slammed the door shut and rushed for the bathroom where we kept the only highly flammable substances we owned.

Harry was kicking up a fearful row, thumping and kicking at the door, but miraculously the little latch held.

Returning with some dusters I spread them out and slid them under the space between the door and the floor, poured the kerosene and methylated spirits on them, took the matches off the telephone table and set the whole lot alight.

By the time the neighbours and the police arrived there was quite a merry little blaze going. Unfortunately there was as much on my side of the cupboard as on Harry's, and by the time I had got Alistair untied the house was full of smoke and we could hardly breathe. We watched from the street as the fire brigade arrived amid the most awful din, and firemen clutching axes ran in and out. Small boys in striped pyjamas kept getting in the way, asking excitedly how the fire had started. Harry was rescued by the firemen and then arrested by the police, who drove him away coughing in the paddy-wagon.

People I had never seen before appeared in their night clothes offering us cups of tea and a bed for the night, but by the time all the smoke had cleared, literally and figuratively, Zoltan, Tim and Peter had come back. Zoltan went over to speak to the people who owned Charlie. I don't know what he said exactly but they kept nodding and smiling at me whenever they caught my eye so I took it I was forgiven.

After we had told Peter and Zoltan what had happened they took the opportunity to tell us that they had got Leo Thompson and the real Mr X behind bars at last.

"They'll be looking for a new assistant commissioner. Perhaps I should apply?" Peter laughed, trying to make a joke of it, but he was looking at Zoltan intently.

"Of course!" Zoltan said, slapping his friend on the back. Peter smiled.

Zoltan invited all of us to sleep at his parents' house and although I would not really have chosen to meet my future parents-in-law wearing a torn night-dress and with my eye-lashes singed, I couldn't really sleep in the house reeking of smoke as it was.

I expected Zoltan's mother to come swanning out to meet us with her blond hair piled on top of her head and wearing a diaphanous negligee, saying, "Come in, darlink." In fact, she was a little dark dumpy woman who wore thick pebble glasses and a man's dressing-gown. As soon as we arrived she ran nervously about just like my own mother faced with unexpected visitors, hauling sheets and pillow-slips out of cupboards and muttering to herself.

Zoltan put two camp-beds in one of the bedrooms, saying, "You'll have to share with my grandmother." Tim, Alistair and Peter were to sleep in Zoltan's room in sleeping bags. I was starting to think Peter didn't have a home of his own.

Zoltan's father, a calm, even phlegmatic man, plied us with home-made wine, in case any of us were suffering from shock, he told us. When Christine and I couldn't stay awake any longer, Zoltan introduced us to his grandmother, who, he had earlier informed us, was ninety-six. She was sitting up in bed reading, wearing a very pretty woollen shawl around her shoulders. She could tell I was admiring it.

"My daughter-in-law made it for me. You don't think the colour's too old for me, do you?" she enquired anxiously. Christine and I exchanged glances before we reassured her on that point. While we got undressed, Zoltan's grandmother chattered on.

"You know, I was followed home by a sailor last week."

We turned off the light to hide our smiles. I knew I was going to like Zoltan's family.

In the morning Mrs Baker hung over the stove like a servant, making us huge quantities of pancakes. Considering she had never heard of me before, she took the news of our engagement quite in her stride.

"One less to cook for," she declared with an elaborate Hungarian wave of her hand.

Mr Baker read out of the paper to us about the fire the night before, and even more importantly the headlined story about the drug-ring being smashed by a combined Australian-New Zealand police operation.

According to Zoltan, Mrs Livingston had been released from the hospital and was being returned to Rata House that morning, so after we had been to my place and Christine and I had got dressed, we all called in to see her.

Mrs Livingston had news of her own. With an attempt at

nonchalance she told us she was going for a trip to America shortly. Both the elderly gentleman she had befriended at Stewart Island and Mrs Roberts had invited her to stay with them and she had taken them at their word.

"When I come back I intend on selling Rata House and moving into a town house."

"Oh, Mrs Livingston, don't sell it. It's too beautiful to let go."

After a moment's reflection she said, "I'll tell you what I am going to do. I'll sell it to you and Zoltan for the price of a good town house."

"Really, do you mean it?" I asked.

"I'd like you to have it. I can't stay here rattling around in this big place all on my own, and I don't want strangers to have it."

"Oh, when it's ours you can come and visit us all the time," I said in a great rush of enthusiasm.

"I intend to," she said with a smile. "Why else do you think I'm letting you have it so cheaply!"

While the others stayed talking to Mrs Livingston, Zoltan and I slipped outside to view the grounds and walk hand-in-hand under the rose-covered trellis, like two lovers.

www.ingramcontent.com/pod-product-compliance
Lightning Source LLC
Chambersburg PA
CBHW031333060726

47590CB00007B/2451